Southern elegance

"So," Desha said, "how's business here? The store kind of looks...like a funeral parlor, doesn't it?" She sucked in her breath. She had thought that, but she hadn't meant to *say* it. "Well, not that bad," she retracted soothingly, "but it is pretty quiet."

Bryce frowned. "Don't you think you might give it a chance?" he asked dryly. "Aren't you a bit premature with your death announcement? You've been here what—two minutes? The store isn't even open to customers yet."

"But business could be better?" she asked.

"Are you doing a survey, or are *you* planning to dramatically increase business?"

"Would you *like* for me to?"

He had to grin at her incredible confidence. She was so terribly cocky that he couldn't even get angry. "By all means, Desha. Step right in and make me a fortune."

"All right," she said solemnly. "I'll do my best."

Dear Reader:

The spirit of the Silhouette Romance Homecoming Celebration lives on as each month we bring you six books by continuing stars!

And we have a galaxy of stars planned for 1988. In the coming months, we're publishing romances by many of your favorite authors such as Annette Broadrick, Sondra Stanford and Brittany Young. Beginning in January, Debbie Macomber has written a trilogy designed to cure any midwinter blues. And that's not all—during the summer, Diana Palmer presents her most engaging heros and heroines in a trilogy that will be sure to capture your heart.

Your response to these authors and other authors of Silhouette Romances has served as a touchstone for us, and we're pleased to bring you more books with Silhouette's distinctive medley of charm, wit and—above all—romance.

I hope you enjoy this book and the many stories to come. Come home to romance—for always!

Sincerely,

Tara Hughes
Senior Editor
Silhouette Books

BRENDA TRENT

Cupid's
Error

Silhouette Romance

Published by Silhouette Books New York

America's Publisher of Contemporary Romance

SILHOUETTE BOOKS
300 E. 42nd St., New York, N.Y. 10017

Copyright © 1987 by Brenda Himrod

ISBN: 0-373-08540-0

First Silhouette Books printing November 1987

America's Publisher of Contemporary Romance

Printed in the U.S.A.

Books by Brenda Trent

Silhouette Romance

Rising Star # 56
Winter Dreams # 74
A Stranger's Wife #110
Run from Heartache #161
Runaway Wife #193
Steal Love Away #245
Hunter's Moon #266
Bewitched by Love #423
A Better Man #488
Hearts on Fire #506
Cupid's Error #540

Silhouette Special Edition

Stormy Affair #51

Silhouette Desire

Without Regrets #130

BRENDA TRENT

has a life right out of a romance. She followed her heart from Virginia to California, where she met and married the man of her dreams. With his encouragement she gave up working to concentrate on another dream, writing, and we are proud to introduce her work through Silhouette Romances.

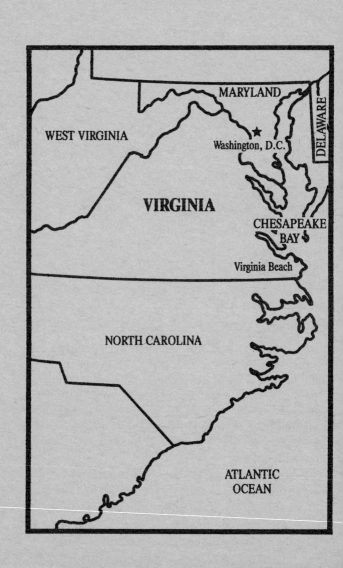

Chapter One

Desha smiled as she left 58 East and headed toward Virginia Beach on 44 East. It was a perfect day: blue sky, sunshine, tall green trees, and the ocean nearby. Everything was going splendidly, and she was glad she had selected Virginia.

In her twenty-three years, this was the third state in which she'd decided to locate—the second one since she was eighteen. She hadn't been able to find the right spot, the suitable spot, to settle down and live her life, but suddenly she had that tickle of anticipation. The vibes were good; she sensed that Virginia was going to be home for her.

Abruptly, she saw the sign for the toll road. "Oh, no!" she muttered as she tried to steady the old tank of a car with one hand and rummage around in her huge shoulder bag for money. She couldn't seem to find her wallet in all the debris cluttering the bag.

"Shucks!" She bit it out as she glanced up. Now she was in the lane that said Correct Change Only. She couldn't find a quarter, and she was quickly losing patience. The newest state she'd decided to call home was not treating her too kindly at the moment.

"So what are they going to do with me if I don't have a quarter?" she asked herself aloud. "Shoot me? Send the police after me?"

She thought she was being cavalier about it, but when she actually stopped before the basket, she didn't know what to do. There was a red light stopping her.

"What rotten luck," she groaned. She glanced in the rearview mirror at all the traffic behind her, then looked at the toll booths on each side. There were many; some with attendants who could make change.

Desha felt a short moment of panic. She couldn't go back and she couldn't go forward. She was tired from traveling all day and couldn't seem to think clearly.

Finally she dragged the wallet from the depths of her bag and pulled out one of the few pieces of paper money she had left. She put her open wallet on the top of the bag and stared down at the dollar she removed. Briefly, she considered darting over to another toll booth and asking for change.

The man behind her blew his horn, causing her to jump. She looked in her rearview mirror at the silver Mercedes.

Desha stared at the driver for a moment, then impulsively climbed out of her car and ran back to his. "Listen, we're going to be here all day if you don't help me," she said with what appeared to be incredible calmness and arrogance. "I don't have a quarter. I've got a dollar if you could make change for me."

Bryce Gerrard was so surprised by the young woman that he stared at her with raised brows. He had lived in Virginia Beach all his thirty years, with the exception of the four he spent in the Army, and he had thought he'd seen all kinds of tourists and wackos, but this one appeared to be a newer, bolder breed.

"I'm not a cash register," he drawled in his deep Virginia accent. "You should have gone to a toll booth that had an attendant."

Someone behind Bryce blew his horn with a heavy hand and Desha looked down the line, her dark brown eyes flashing impatiently. The other lines were crawling on past the booths; the drivers far back in this line were switching lanes dangerously fast, trying to avoid being delayed.

"I followed the crowd," she said firmly when her gaze again rested on Bryce. "People are getting hostile behind you. Now are you going to be nice or not?"

A small smile tugged at the corners of Bryce's mouth at her question. He quickly scanned her outfit.

The late May temperature was in the eighties and the young woman wore a bright, blousy coat with padded shoulders over a calf-length dress. Her color preference clearly leaned toward the dramatic, for the dress amplified the purple pattern in the coat. Her hair was short, black and windblown. She wore long earrings.

Desha couldn't miss the curious way he looked at her, and she sensed his disapproval. Well, one look at *him* and she knew from his conservative attire that he didn't know the first thing about fashionable clothing—*men's*, let alone women's. Let him stare. She didn't care what he thought as long as he lent her a quarter so they both could get on with life.

Her car probably had no air-conditioning, Bryce surmised, suddenly feeling a rush of sympathy as he met her eyes. He handed her his quarter and raised up to search his pocket for another one. He would be the one in trouble if he didn't have change.

"Thanks," the woman said, her attractive face now wreathed in smiles. "Tell me where, and I'll return this."

"Consider it a gift. Just get in your car and move," Bryce said, listening to the angry horn-blowers behind him.

He found a quarter and sat in his car, shaking his head as he watched the woman walk back to the disaster of a vehicle she drove. Her long T-shirt dress swayed rhythmically against slender legs wrapped in the straps of her lavender Roman sandals. The sight was somehow provocative, and Bryce shifted his attention to the rest of her clothing.

Her baggy coat with its padded shoulders clung to her back; a lavender scarf trailed behind her. He found himself wondering what kind of figure she was hiding behind those loose, flamboyant clothes. One of her earrings caught the sun and shone brightly as she bent to climb back into her car. Bryce was momentarily mesmerized by the lightning-like design as the earring danced an impromptu jig behind the woman's ear.

"Lord, help us all," he said, making himself stop staring at her. How did people like that survive? What on earth did someone like her do with her life? He wished his mother could see this one—his mother owned *Southern Elegance* and *Southern Pride*, two of the most exclusive women's shops in the state.

Desha sighed in relief as she tossed the quarter in the basket and restarted the old red car. It coughed a couple of times and sputtered.

"Now don't you give me trouble, Betty!" she cried. "Let's just get out of here."

Miraculously, the ancient car seemed to hear her. With a lurch, Desha drove away from the toll booth. Getting in the far right lane, she glanced back in her mirror in time to see the man in the silver Mercedes pull into a faster lane of traffic.

"Imperialist!" she accused.

Then she began to laugh. She didn't know why she had called him that. Because he looked so rich and self-assured? Because he had that fancy car? Because he had such a dashing air about him, despite his too-conventional clothing? Or was it because he appeared to have reached a position in life that she was still struggling for?

She chuckled. He had looked so taken aback when she went to his car. But he had given her a quarter. And yes, he did look like a cash register—or at least like he owned one.

Still grinning at the memory, she watched as he changed lanes a few cars up ahead of her. The afternoon traffic was sluggish and clearly the man was eager to get where he was going.

Suddenly the old car engine shut off. Just like that. "Don't do this to me, Betty!" Desha cried. "Please, please, please."

As the car slowed down, she tried desperately to restart it while the people behind her once again blew maddeningly, as though she were doing this on purpose.

"Oh, go on by!" she cried to them in general as she coasted over to the side of the road, waving her hand out the open window to indicate that they should go around her. Only by God's grace did she manage to get far enough out of the way to stop safely. She thanked her lucky stars, if she still had any, that she'd been in the slowest lane, and the traffic itself wasn't moving very fast.

Bryce looked into his rearview mirror to see what the newest commotion was all about. "I should have known," he said aloud, when he saw the old car slowing down traffic. "First she has no quarter, now she has car trouble."

He moved ahead a few more feet, but again glanced back at Desha's car, watching as she miraculously managed to get off the highway.

He shook his head. She was a colorfully dressed, bold young stranger. She had nothing to do with him. She was certainly not his responsibility. He had done his good deed for the day. He glanced back a final time, seeing the young woman step out of the car and look up and down the highway.

"Hell," he muttered unhappily as he changed to the far right lane, looking for the next exit. He didn't know why he was doing this. He glanced down at his watch. Juliette would be wondering what happened to him. He was sure to be late for their date, and they were doubling with Lew and Alicia tonight.

Desha kicked the front tire with a sandaled foot as she stood out on the side of the highway, trying to decide what to do now. Then she bent down and patted the place she had kicked. She knew she shouldn't blame the car.

It had gotten her from Taos, New Mexico, where she had spent her first eighteen years, to New York City, where she had struggled futilely to become a Broadway star, to South Carolina where she had sunk every dime she'd had into a clothing store of her own.

She had gone broke in the venture, unfortunately, but at least she'd tried. She wanted to be successful by the time she was thirty. South Carolina hadn't helped her with her goal, so she decided to try her fortune elsewhere.

Some fortune, she thought, briefly wondering if she could sell Betty for junk and get enough money to stay afloat until she found work. She felt guilty, as if she were thinking of killing an old friend.

"Never mind," she murmured to the car. "I won't resort to that. I'm not sure what I'll do, but I won't do that. I just hope you don't cost too much to repair."

An older, navy-colored truck pulled up and parked in front of her car, and she smiled gently to herself. "Maybe our luck is changing," she murmured to Betty.

"Trouble, miss?" a man called out.

Desha nodded. "The car just stopped while I was driving along," she explained. "I don't know what happened."

"Want me to take a look?" he asked.

"I'd sure appreciate it." Desha gave him her best smile.

She watched as the tall, lanky young man in worn jeans, a thin blue shirt and old boots walked quickly toward her. She told herself that he looked as poor as she was.

Wasn't that the way of it? No one else had even glanced in her direction, but this man, who probably knew as much about hard times as she did, had taken the time to try to help her.

He climbed into the car and turned the key in the ignition. For a single, bright moment, Desha hoped for a miracle, but nothing happened.

"She's dead," the man called, his cool blue eyes meeting Desha's when he glanced out the window at her. Desha noticed for the first time how hard his burnished, sun-lined face looked and how rough his voice was.

"Do you have any tools?" he asked.

"A few in the trunk. I'll get them."

He handed her the car keys. While Desha went around to the rear of the car, she expected him to raise the hood. When he didn't, she looked into the car. Saints above, he was taking her wallet!

"Stop that! Don't you dare do that!" she cried, racing around to the passenger's side of the car. She grabbed her bag through the open window, but the man had already taken her wallet. He slid out of her car and ran toward his truck.

"Thief, stop!" she cried frantically. He had every dime she had in the world and all her identification. Wildly, she chased after him, her carpetbag bouncing on her arm. "You stop! Come back here and fight like a man!"

He turned suddenly and shoved her with one long, muscled arm, sending her sprawling to the dirt, her purse emptying its myriad contents as Desha tumbled roughly to the ground.

She watched in impotent rage as the old dark blue truck joined the rest of the traffic and roared off down the road. How dare he rob her! *She* had earned that money!

"You monster!" she yelled, her fist raised in anger. Oh, if only she could have grabbed him before he shoved her, she would have taught him a lesson or two. She had let the element of surprise be her undoing. Tears of fury gathered in her eyes and she looked down at all the odds and ends that had fallen from her purse.

She was so lost in her outrage that she didn't hear Bryce's car pull behind hers and stop. When she looked up from her unladylike position, her brown eyes glistening with unshed tears, he was standing before her.

"What happened now?" he asked. "Are you all right?"

She hadn't realized how tall and handsome he was when she asked him for the quarter. Her eyes briefly skimmed down his angular face with those piercing blue eyes, black brows and short black hair. His cool reserve fueled her anger.

"Do I look all right?" she barked, humiliation coloring her cheeks. "What do you want? The last man took everything." She gestured wildly to the things strewn around her. "That's all that's left."

Bryce frowned. He had no way of knowing what had happened. "What do you mean?"

"I mean he robbed me! That's what I mean." She pointed down the road with a quivering finger. Her voice was just as unsteady. "That man in that blue truck pulled over here like a good Samaritan, climbed in my car and took my wallet."

"I'm sorry," Bryce said, his voice low.

"You aren't," Desha refuted, venting her frustration on him. "You don't even know me. You don't care what happens to me. Get in your fancy car and drive on."

"Do you really want me to?" he asked, his eyes holding hers challengingly. He deplored crime in any form, and it always seemed especially unfair when those who had the least were victimized. Unless appearances were deceiving, this woman had very little.

When Desha looked up at him with those dark, moist eyes, framed by a thick fringe of black lashes, Bryce inexplicably felt his heartbeat increase.

She drew in her breath, embarrassed to find herself in this position. "No," she answered contritely, "I don't think I do."

He held out a hand to help her up, and when she slipped her slender fingers into his, Bryce noticed the long nails painted red, and the rings on her fingers. The faint scent of her lilac perfume teased his nostrils.

Desha felt a tiny thrill race over her when her fingers touched Bryce's. For a moment she was taken aback by the good vibrations she felt. Ridiculous, she told herself. This man wasn't even her type, not that she had decided what her type was, but it certainly wasn't a magazine-ad perfect man like this one. The tumble had confused her senses.

"Thanks," she said, quickly disengaging her hand when she was on her feet. She hurriedly brushed herself off, then looked into the man's eyes.

"I should warn you that I don't aim to put up with being ripped off again. I *can* defend myself. You're here to help me, aren't you?"

He smiled at her bluster and bravado. Did she really think he would be here for any other purpose? Did she really think she had *anything* he wanted?

"I'm going to try," he said. He held out his hand again. "My name is Bryce Gerrard."

"Desha Deserra," she said, closing her fingers around his in a firm shake. It happened again; those little tingles ran up and down her arm.

"Desha Deserra," he repeated. "That's some name."

Desha grinned a little, her smile lighting up her dark eyes. "Do you like it?"

He nodded, and did his best not to roll his eyes heavenward. "Not bad. Not bad."

"Actually," she said, her voice taking on a serious tone, "my name is really Desha Smith, but when I was in New York to try my hand at show business, I needed a stage name." She glanced away. "I seem to have more of a business head than an artist's." Her eyes met his again. "What I mean is that I'll be a bigger success in the financial world than on a stage."

Good heavens, Bryce thought to himself, a stage name and she'd chosen a tongue twister like Desha Deserra. He tried his best not to indicate his misgivings about her success in either world. Yet, as he looked at her, he had the feeling that she *was* on stage and that she had every intention in the world of getting proper notice.

"Desha's a pretty name," he said. "Is that real?"

"Oh, yes. My mother named me that because she wanted something unusual. She reasoned that it would make me feel unique, that it would give me an edge on becoming a star."

"I see," he said, clearing his throat. She was definitely unique. "Well, why don't I see if I can get your car started," he said. He held out his hand for the keys. Desha spied them on the ground where they had fallen and picked them up.

This time she was alert, waiting to see what would happen when Bryce touched her. It happened again, those shivers up and down her spine. Even she couldn't ignore a third reaction, but she didn't know what to make of it. She gazed up at the sun. Maybe it was the heat.

Bryce climbed into the car and turned the key in the ignition. Predictably, nothing happened. He tried several times to get the car started, but to no avail. Finally he got out of the car and went around in front to open the hood.

After a few minutes of jiggling parts, he shook his head. "It looks hopeless," he said. "I'll give you a ride to the police station, and you can report the theft of your wallet, explain your situation and maybe get a wrecker out here for your car."

"I can't afford a wrecker," she said. Bryce didn't miss the way she lifted her chin and stiffened her back proudly. "My wallet is gone, remember?"

He shifted uneasily and told himself that he should have known better than to come back and get involved with this highway hazard.

"They'll know how to help you at the station," he said. "Did you get the truck's license number?"

"No. When would I have had time to do that? I was too busy defending myself and my property."

"I see." Bryce bent down to avoid the vulnerable look in her eyes. He hadn't expected it. She was only about five and a half feet tall, but she was so feisty and colorful that she appeared taller, almost invincible somehow.

"Here, let me help you pick up your belongings."
He began to gather up an incredible array of lip-
sticks, eye colors and sample perfume bottles.

Desha bent down beside him, quickly grabbing for
the things he had missed, including pens, paper, maps,
and a package of crumbled crackers.

When he straightened, he helped her stuff the items
back in her purse. "So you're from South Carolina,"
he said, making conversation as he noticed her license plate.

"By way of New York," she said as she slung her
bag over her shoulder.

"Right. The stage name." Bryce smiled at her.

He stared at her huge old carpetbag. Ridiculously
large and multicolored, it managed to blend in with
the rest of her attire and jewelry. He scanned her face
and wondered what it looked like without the makeup she wore. He saw that her earrings really were designed to look like lightning bolts, and he noticed that
she had small, delicate ears.

As he gazed at the colorful woman, he suddenly
tried to imagine what Juliette, cool, blond and re-
fined, would look like in some of the distinctive garb.
Juliette! He had better hurry or he was really going to
be late.

"You'll want to get your luggage, and we'll be on
our way to the police station," he said, indicating his
car.

Having no other choice, Desha reached into the
back seat of her car and pulled out a bulky purple
backpack. She slung it over her shoulder, rolled up the
car windows, then started walking toward Bryce's vehicle.

"Is that all your baggage?" he asked.

She nodded. "I travel light."

"I see." He wondered if she were wearing the rest of her clothing. Only heaven knew what was under that big jacket. He picked up his pace; he wanted to get on with his evening.

Desha followed him, but she glanced longingly at Betty. She'd had to have many repairs done on the car in the four years she had owned it, but she'd never had to walk off and abandon Betty by the side of the road. She slid into the cool, dark interior of Bryce's sleek silver machine, then looked over her shoulder once more at her own cumbersome car.

"Just a minute," Bryce said, retrieving something from his back seat.

Desha saw that it was a Vehicle Disabled sign. She watched as Bryce went over to her car and placed the boldly lettered sign in the rear window. Her dark eyes skimmed along Bryce's muscled form, and she found herself thinking how attractive he was. She couldn't help but wonder if he were rich, and if he were married. In his gray striped summer suit, he looked very classy—conservative, yes, but definitely classy.

"Classy, smassy," she grumbled aloud.

She didn't care if he were rich, and she certainly didn't care if he were married. She was going to make her own way, make her own mark in the world. And, by the blue heavens above, she intended to make a bold mark!

"That should alert people to the danger of the car parked off the side of the road," Bryce said when he joined Desha.

She nodded, then watched as he started the engine. It roared to life and Bryce blended in with the surging traffic as easily as if the road were totally empty. Desha noticed his smooth, tanned hands with their neatly manicured nails. He wore no rings.

"Are you married?" she asked. She hadn't meant to, but she *did* wonder, and she had asked before she could stop herself.

Bryce glanced over at her, then shook his head. "No. Are you?"

She shrugged off the question. "No. I'm not ready to marry yet."

Grinning, he said, "You're not? How and when does one decide these things? I suppose you reason that you're too young, and probably rightfully so, but I thought love was the determining factor."

She looked at him. "I'm not too young. I was twenty-three years old on April tenth, but the stars haven't lined up right for me to consider marriage yet. Those things are actually decided with the help of an astrology chart."

"With an astrology chart?" he repeated incredulously.

She nodded. "After all, marriage is a lifetime adventure. I'm an Aries, of course. We're leaders, movers and shakers, headstrong, determined. Creative, too. We have to be very careful who we permanently align ourselves with. I consult my horoscope daily to determine my course."

"I see," Bryce murmured, doing his best to keep from smiling. She looked like a mover and shaker all right, and he could well picture this woman consulting her horoscope for her life's adventures. He had a feeling she had some incredible ones.

"What did it show for today?" he couldn't resist asking as he maneuvered the car through traffic.

Desha frowned. "This is a good day for traveling or I wouldn't have traveled."

Her frown deepened, and Bryce found himself noticing how pretty her features were. Her eyes were large and well-shaped, her brows exquisitely winged, her nose small but fine, her lips full with a Cupid's bow.

He looked away. "Well, someone must have gotten her stars crossed when she advised you," he said. "I don't call having your car break down and getting robbed a good day for traveling."

Desha was pensive a moment. "No," she admitted reluctantly. "But maybe something good will come of it," she quickly added.

He looked at her. "Like what?"

She shrugged her shoulders under all the padding. "I don't know," she mused.

"No," he said. "I didn't think you did."

He glanced at his watch again as he approached the police station. He was already ten minutes late for his date with Juliette. Next time he was going to remind himself not to play the good Samaritan.

Of course, he could just walk away now and leave the woman, but it didn't seem like the decent thing to do. She had made him feel guilty with that statement about not caring about her.

It, like all guilt, was ridiculous he thought. After all, he'd given her the quarter and he'd returned when he saw her pull off the highway. Now that he'd come this far, he might as well wait until she talked to the police.

"Do you have friends in Virginia Beach?" he asked Desha as they walked into the building.

She shook her head. "Not yet, but I make friends very easily."

He smiled. "I'll bet you do." He could almost visualize the vibrant assortment of strangers she would attract.

She glanced at him, wondering what he meant by that comment, then gave her attention to the man at the desk.

Bryce stood by listening, as she explained what had happened then was directed to another man. As she gave her report, he couldn't help but notice the way she gestured with her ringed hands as she talked, often adding a qualifier to her statements.

He was nearly hypnotized as he listened to her animated description of handling the robber and the attack. He hadn't been of the opinion she had fared as well as she was indicating to the policeman. Bryce saw the curiosity in the man's eyes as he glanced from Desha to him.

Lost in his own thoughts, he didn't realize that Desha had finished her statement. She turned to him and held out her hand.

"Thanks a lot, Bryce. I'll be going now. I'll still send you that quarter if you'll tell me where, and I'll pay you for your time and gas too."

"That won't be necessary, thank you anyway." Bryce walked along beside her as she headed toward the door. "Where are you going? I didn't hear you ask the policeman about housing. Aren't you broke?"

"Yes, I am. But only temporarily," she added. "I've been broke before, and I've managed."

Bryce was curious. "How? Where will you sleep? What will you eat?"

She shrugged. When she left home at eighteen, prodded by dreams and dissatisfaction, she had promised herself that she wouldn't ask anything of anybody. Pride had kept her from asking the policeman for a handout. This was a difficult situation. Still, something would come to her. It always did.

"I haven't decided," Desha told Bryce, tilting her head at him. With all these hotels, maybe she could get a job as a maid or cook and get a room and meals.

He pressed his lips into a tight line. This foolish female spoke as if she had every choice in the world, as if she were deciding which fancy hotel to grace with her presence.

"You don't already have a job, do you?"

She shook her head. "Not yet."

He reached for his wallet and pulled out a hundred-dollar bill. "Here, maybe this will tide you over."

Her dark eyes flashed as she brushed his hand aside. "Thanks, but I don't take charity." She pushed open the door and strode out onto the sidewalk, her dress brushing against her legs as she walked.

Bryce crumpled the bill in his hand and followed her. "You don't?" he asked, exasperated because of her recklessly proud attitude. "What was the quarter?"

She opened her mouth wide in protest. "It wasn't *charity*! That quarter was a loan. I told you I wanted to return it."

Bryce sighed tiredly and looked at his watch again. Twenty minutes late. He didn't have time to argue. He didn't have time for this unpredictable woman. He didn't know why he was standing here doing this.

"Consider this a loan," he said, pulling out his wallet again. "Return it to me at this address." He held both the card and the rumpled hundred-dollar bill out to Desha.

She took the card, but not the money. "Thanks again, Bryce. See you around." Then she walked away.

For an incredulous moment, Bryce started after her. He didn't know why he had the urge to charge after her and shake her until she realized how foolishly she was behaving. She was nothing to him. Angrily, he shoved the hundred-dollar bill into his shirt pocket, strode to his car and climbed in.

Chapter Two

Damned fool woman,'' Bryce said as he started his car and pulled away from the curb. He glanced back over his shoulder and saw Desha looking up and down the street as if she were trying to decide what her next move would be.

He carelessly shrugged one shoulder. He had done his part and more. Refusing to look at her again, he drove off.

When he reached the bend in the road, he pulled over to the side and drew in a steadying breath. What would the little fool do? Where would she stay? As incredible as it seemed, he was worried about her. She was kooky and defiant, but she was vulnerable. Where could a woman like that go?

He suddenly remembered that one of the women who worked in his mother's shop was quitting to get married. He oversaw all the family business, and he would be the one finding a replacement for Mira.

Maybe— He quickly disabused himself of the forming thought. Even if Desha had the proper training, he couldn't hire her to work at *Southern Elegance*. The very thought was ridiculous. The customers would run away if that outrageous woman tried to advise them on the proper attire.

But maybe there was something else she could do in the shop, something temporary until she could get on her feet. Perhaps she could help Judy at the main office with the bookkeeping. The tourist season was almost here. He could use that as an excuse. He doubted that Desha knew much about bookkeeping, but Judy could teach her for a couple of weeks. And who knows? Maybe Desha would even learn something.

Abruptly, he slammed his fist down on the steering wheel. Why was he doing this? He had to get to a phone and call Juliette. She, Lew and Alicia had probably already left the house. They had reservations for dinner.

He started the car again and whipped around the corner, but he was heading back to the police station. Desha was still standing there on the street.

He pressed a button to roll down the passenger window. "Do you know anything about bookkeeping?" he asked, leaning down so that he could meet her eyes.

She didn't seem surprised to see him. "I took it in high school, but I hated it. Why?"

"I oversee some businesses, including my mother's dress shops. We need some help in accounts. Are you interested?"

"No," she said, to his annoyance, "but I'll help out in the shops if you need someone. I had a shop of my own in South Carolina."

"You did?" he asked, sounding doubtful.

"Yes."

"And?" He waited for her to explain.

She shrugged. "I went broke." She grinned a little in embarrassment. "I told you I'd been broke before. But it wasn't my fault," she added. "If only I'd had more money and more time, I would have made a success of that business. I know I would have."

Bryce briefly closed his eyes and ran his hands through his hair. His mother would die if she knew what he was contemplating. He exhaled wearily. Maybe he could have Bernice discreetly talk to Desha about the proper way to dress for a shop like *Southern Elegance*.

"Yes, I need someone in one shop."

"What does it pay?" she asked.

Bryce resisted an urge to slam his fist down on the steering wheel again. The woman was *desperate*. Didn't she understand that? She was broke, and she was without a car. She was in no position to haggle over salary, especially when he was only doing her a favor.

"Get in," he said. "I'll discuss salary with you tomorrow. Right now I'm late for an important engagement. I know a reasonable motel where you can stay, within walking distance of the shop." He held up his hand before she could give him a rebuttal. "I'll give you a salary advance, and we'll work out everything tomorrow. All right?"

Desha grinned at him as she climbed into the car, baring one slender leg before she covered it with her dress. "All right," she said. "See, I told you something would work out. It always does. Oh, and you won't be sorry. You'll see. I'll have that business of your mother's booming in no time.''

''What the—''

Bryce smothered an oath and pulled back out into traffic. He didn't know who was the craziest—him or her. He hadn't said his mother's business wasn't booming.

He frowned. The fact of the matter was that sales had been down in the last two quarters. But *Southern Elegance* was still definitely showing a profit, and if financial experts couldn't increase business, this dippy female sure couldn't!

Desha studied the handsome man out of the corner of her eye. She had seen his type before. Mr. Stuffed Shirt. Mr. Self-Important. Him with his *mother's* shops. He probably hadn't earned a dime of his own in his life! Well, he didn't impress her.

She smiled a little. He didn't impress her with his money, but she had to admit that he was good-looking. She had always liked tall men, and he had to be at least six feet. He was also athletic-looking, despite that stiffly conservative air about him.

''Exactly what is it you do for a living?'' she asked, turning to face him.

Bryce looked at her, then back at the street. ''I manage the family business, oversee the properties, sit on the board, that kind of thing.''

''Oh,'' she said, ''that kind of thing.'' She told herself that the family must be richer than she had thought for Bryce to spend all his time handling finances. ''What sign are you?'' she asked, frowning.

''I haven't the slightest idea,'' he replied dryly.

''Well, when were you born?''

''May seventh.''

"Taurus," she murmured. That explained it. Taurus, the Bull—stubborn, financially aware, security-conscious, cautious, reserved, *impossibly* practical.

"Here we are," he said, pulling up in front of an older, adequate-looking hotel about four blocks from the beach.

Desha pursed her lips together as she assessed the building. It looked fine. She had stayed in many that were much less appealing. She glanced around. She liked the area. She could almost smell the ocean although Bryce had the windows closed and the air-conditioning on.

The vibes were good. Businesses were interspersed with hotels and restaurants. She could stay here. But impulsively she decided that she simply didn't want Bryce making her housing decisions for her. She didn't let anybody pick out a place as important as her living quarters—unless of course, she thought, it was her astrologer.

"It's not close enough to the beach," she declared. "I believe I'll get a room at one of the others, maybe right on the water." She waved her hand vaguely in the direction of some of the tallest, most luxurious hotels on the strip.

Bryce's jaw muscles tightened almost imperceptibly. "You can't afford them." He shut off the car engine and turned to look at her. "Unless, of course, you have some money secreted away somewhere that you haven't told me about. Those hotel rooms cost seventy to a hundred or more a night."

Desha liked the way he had said *secreted away*. It sounded so polished. It also sounded like a typical money-minded Taurus. "I don't have any money stashed away, but I want to stay on the beach," she insisted.

At patience's end, Bryce declared, "I don't have time for this. Do what you want, but I have to go." He reached for another card and pulled out two one-hundred-dollar bills.

"This is the shop address." Pointing down the street, he said, "It's the tan building. Show up by nine in the morning—if you can manage to do that. Here's a salary advance."

Ignoring the money, Desha gazed in the direction where he pointed. The building looked as she imagined it would—sedate and stuffy. *Southern Elegance*, she mused. What else for this man? Still, she certainly needed the job, and he needed a clerk.

She took the card and money and opened her car door. "Since you need somebody, it's the least I can do. I'll be there." She made herself smile brightly. After all, he *had* gone well out of his way to help her. "Thanks a lot, Bryce. You've been awfully nice."

He nodded and Desha stepped back, watching as he put the car in gear and pulled away. When he was gone, she stared at the hotel he had suggested. She really would like to be on the water, but two hundred dollars wouldn't go far at seventy dollars a night. Besides, she wanted to get Betty off the highway.

Adjusting her backpack and shoulder bag, she set off in the direction of *Southern Elegance*. She would check it out, then find suitable, reasonable housing. She simply couldn't make herself take the hotel Bryce had suggested. He had already exerted too much influence over her life by virtue of her circumstances.

* * *

Bryce turned his car over to the parking attendant and hurried inside the restaurant. He was forty minutes late. There had been no point in trying to phone Juliette. The maître d' recognized him and beamed broadly.

"Your party is this way, Mr. Gerrard. They're waiting for you."

"Thank you."

Bryce followed him through a long, black-and-white marbled hallway to a room luxuriously decorated with black-clothed tables and stiffly starched white napkins. Juliette saw him and waved a hand in recognition.

"Sorry I'm late," Bryce said as he slipped into the plush chair at Juliette's side. The tall, chic blonde was such a contrast to Desha that it took Bryce a moment to adjust.

"Darling, what happened? I've been concerned."

As he leaned over and kissed one fair cheek, he glimpsed the small diamond earring in Juliette's pink ear, and he had a sudden vision of Desha's lightning bolts dancing in the sun.

"I was delayed on the road," he explained. Somehow he just didn't think Juliette would understand Desha's plight.

"An accident?" she asked, her cultured voice rising slightly.

Bryce had a sudden vision of Desha and her old car. Both reminded him of accidents. "Car trouble," he said, not lying, but not quite telling the truth.

"Are you driving the Mercedes?"

He nodded.

"Well, I'd certainly speak to Raymond about that," Juliette said indignantly. "You've only had that car a month."

"Mmm-hmm," he said distractedly.

He wondered where Desha had decided to stay. He pushed back the thought. It was ridiculous for him to devote his time to that woman. This was his world, where he belonged, among people of his own kind.

"So, how are you, Lew? Alicia?"

Desha found a small hotel across the street from the beach, a little past the busiest part of the strip, about seven blocks from *Southern Elegance*. Although she railed against any restricting boundaries, she had to heed the need to curb her rash streak in these times of little money.

The hotel was very reasonable, and she received a discount for registering for a week. She decided that the walk to work would do her good. There were several fast-food restaurants nearby, so she would save money there, too. She had managed to have Betty towed to the hotel parking lot for a small sum, so that was off her mind as well.

Her room was on the fourth floor, and she had a view of the ocean, even though she had to peer around the buildings across the street. She sat down on the bed and patted it. She liked hard beds, and she considered herself fortunate to find one. This hotel would be fine.

She decided to put her few clothes in the closet and drawers. As she unpacked, she glanced out the window. There, right on the street, in broad daylight in his blue truck, was the man who had robbed her!

Flinging down the dress she was holding, Desha raced out into the hall and impatiently rang for the elevator. When it didn't arrive rapidly enough, she hurried to the stairs.

Fairly flying, she raced down the steps two at a time, holding on to the rail for dear life. She'd be darned if that thief was going to spend her money at this beach! She was determined to see justice done, and if that wasn't possible, she was at least determined to see that the man didn't blithely go about his business after he had robbed her!

To her chagrin, when she plunged out onto the street, she couldn't find the truck anywhere. She rushed along, looking up and down the side streets, but the blue truck had vanished. For a moment, she pondered whether or not to call the police. They already had a description of both the man and the truck, but they didn't know that the man was still in the vicinity.

"Rotten luck," she muttered unhappily as she retraced her steps to the hotel. She would call the police and let them know she had seen the man, and she wouldn't quit looking for him herself. He didn't know who he had tangled with. She wasn't going to take this thing lying down. How dare he add insult to injury by remaining right in her neighborhood!

Fuming, she returned to her room and finished unpacking. As she looked around, she told herself that she should count her lucky stars that she had run into Bryce. He had made her life a lot easier by giving her money for this room and giving her a job.

She sighed as she contemplated what to expect at work tomorrow. *Southern Elegance*. What a name. And at the beach yet! Surely there was something catchier. She would think on it during the night. Maybe something would come to her in a dream.

* * *

Desha was up bright and early the next morning. After she had dressed in a blue sleeveless dress with a white underblouse, blue flats and blue earrings, she went to a local fast-food restaurant for breakfast. She ate for less than a dollar, then headed to *Southern Elegance*.

When she had smoothed down one sleeve of her blouse, she opened the door and walked in. It was worse than she'd thought when she peered through the window last night. The walls were tan. The carpet was tan. The dressing rooms were tan. Even the racks and hangers were tan.

A single brown silk dress and two-inch beige heels decorated an ancient mannequin. Rows of purses and belts bordered the large rooms where everything was separated into categories. Rows of blouses, skirts, dresses and coats hung in unimaginative lines.

"Yes? May I help you?"

Desha spun around to meet the inquiring green eyes of the salesclerk. Tall and thirtyish, she was attractive in a haughty kind of way, and she dressed as Desha expected a clerk in this store to dress, expensively and sedately. She was studying Desha with the utmost curiosity evident in her eyes.

"Bryce sent me," Desha said. "I'm the new salesclerk."

The woman couldn't hide her surprise. "I beg your pardon," she murmured. The other salesclerk stepped out from behind the counter, and she and the tall one exchanged glances.

At just that moment, Bryce entered the shop. "Good morning, Bernice. I see you've met Desha."

"Not quite," she said, turning to Bryce, her expression full of bewilderment. "Did I understand her to say that you've hired her?"

"Ah—ah, yes," he said, staring at Desha.

If it was at all possible, she looked more out of place for *Southern Elegance* than she had yesterday. He could see Bernice's face turn pale, and he wondered how she would respond when he suggested that she tactfully try to change Desha's image. As he looked at the primly dressed Bernice, he thought the task suddenly seemed monumental, maybe impossible.

"I'm afraid I don't understand," she said, giving Desha another appraising glance. "She's to work here—in this store—with me?"

Bryce smiled soothingly. "Only temporarily. She needs a job."

"Excuse me," Desha interjected. "What do you mean *only temporarily*? I don't have time to spend on this store if I have no future here."

Bryce tried to keep his temper in check. "You needed a job. I gave you one. We'll have to see how it works out. Neither of us said it was a lifetime commitment." He honestly hadn't counted on her wanting to stay long. She was clearly a wanderer. Besides, he didn't think he could afford to lose that many customers.

Desha walked over to stand before him, her hands on her hips, her expression troubled. "Listen, I hope you don't see this as more of your charity. I don't take charity. You said you *needed* someone in this store. Now, I'm more than willing to help out if you *need* someone, but don't make a place for me just so I can earn your two hundred dollars."

Bryce sighed tiredly. Didn't this woman ever do anything without getting passionate about it? "I do *need* someone," he said. "Mira is getting married."

He gestured to the shorter of the two salesclerks. "She's leaving Friday."

Desha looked at the small, dark woman. "Oh, so you're getting married," she said, smiling. She held out her hand. "Congratulations. I hope you'll be very happy. Marriage isn't for everyone," she added, "so good luck."

Bryce shook his head. Was he really hearing this? He watched as Mira gave Desha a weak handshake and then stepped back. Mira and Bernice must think he had lost his mind.

"So," Desha said, still smiling, "how's business here? The place has the atmosphere of a funeral parlor, doesn't it?"

She sucked in her breath as her eyes widened. She had thought that, but she hadn't meant to *say* it. She supposed she was more nervous than she had realized. After all, she didn't want to insult Bryce after he'd helped her. Being blunt and quick-spoken was a typical Aries trait that frequently got her into trouble. She attempted to guard against it when she remembered. Unfortunately, reticence went against her natural grain and was very hard to remember.

"Well, not that bad," she retracted soothingly, "but it is pretty quiet."

Bryce frowned. "Don't you think you might give it a chance?" he asked dryly. "Aren't you a bit premature with your death announcement? You've been here what—two minutes? The store hasn't even opened for the day yet."

Desha slowly revolved to study the interior once more. "But," she said cautiously, "it is rather understated, rather toned down, don't you think?"

Bryce gazed at Mira, and when he saw that she was doing her best to smother a smile, he glowered at Desha. "Some people use the term 'elegant'," he said. "My mother started with this store more than forty years ago. She helped define it and give it an image—an image that states Southern women are unique and special. We have a very select clientele. And wealthy," he added pointedly. "That makes up for lack of volume."

He groaned to himself. Now he was qualifying his statements. He wasn't generally so easily provoked. Why was he letting this crazy woman come into the shop and stir him up? She would never work out.

Desha was pensive for a moment. "You say that wealth makes up for lack of volume. That does mean that business could be better, doesn't it?" she asked, trying to be more tactful.

Bryce didn't believe this was happening. "Why?" he drawled. "Are you doing a survey or are *you* planning to dramatically increase business?"

Desha slowly looked around again, trying to temper her natural rashness. "The place does have potential," she mused aloud. "And the location is fantastic. You should be doing a great business." She met Bryce's eyes. "Would you *like* me to dramatically increase business?"

He had to grin at her incredible confidence. She was so terribly cocky that he couldn't even get angry. Did she think that *she* could do what Mira and Bernice, what he, his mother and their financial advisors had been unable to do?

The clothing business was like everything else. It had its ups and downs. *Southern Elegance* was in a temporary slump. Business was sure to pick up now that the tourist season was upon them.

He nodded teasingly. "By all means, Desha. Step right in and make me a fortune."

"Do you mean it?" she asked.

His smile broadened. "That's what it's all about, isn't it?"

She nodded thoughtfully. She didn't like to be indebted to anyone. This would give her a way to settle her debt to Bryce, to repay him for helping her.

"All right," she said solemnly. "I'll do my best."

"You do that," he murmured with a smile.

He didn't know why he didn't tell her how brash her behavior was. He supposed he was just too amazed—and, yes, he had to admit it—too amused by the whole thing. She was all of twenty-three, and by her own admission *her* shop had failed. Did she really think she would leave an imprint on *Southern Elegance*?

He smiled at her. "Bernice manages both the Virginia Beach shops, so she will only be here part-time. She'll give you your hours. Mira will help train you, but usually only one salesclerk works during the week, two on Saturday. You are agreeable to working six days, aren't you?"

"Yes."

"Good. Later we'll try to arrange something else. The employees earn a salary here. We don't pay on commission because we think it encourages the clerks to badger the customers to make a sale."

"What is the salary?" Desha asked.

Bryce surprised himself by announcing an amazingly generous sum. He really hadn't intended to pay this stranger so well for clerking for him. The salary just rolled out. He knew how badly she needed money, and he also knew how she felt about charity. He had let those factors influence him, something he never did.

A bit embarrassed, he ignored the look Bernice gave him. Clearly she was surprised by the starting wage, but Bryce had no intention of trying to explain. Desha seemed to mull over the more than ample amount, as though she were trying to decide if she would accept it, which brought on Bryce's ire.

"Fine," she said at last. While she knew it was a generous sum, she would soon have to have more money or find a better paying job. She only had seven years to make her goal.

"I hope I didn't overwhelm you with my generosity," Bryce said a bit sarcastically. The woman simply amazed him with her attitude.

"It'll do for a start," Desha said.

Bryce restrained himself from rolling his eyes heavenward in annoyance. "By the way, you get a substantial employee discount on clothes. Please feel free to purchase a new wardrobe in advance. We'll settle up later."

He smiled at his cleverness. He'd come up with a way to get her to dress more discreetly without blatantly telling her. "That's something you can do to help the shop immediately—buy yourself some new clothes."

Misunderstanding his meaning, Desha laughed playfully. "The clothes I would buy wouldn't make that much difference in the shop's till. Anyway, I just don't think I'm into funeral chic."

The minute the words were out of her mouth, she felt like biting off her tongue. What on earth prompted her to say that? She'd tried to remind herself to think before she spoke, but now she appeared dying to compare the shop to a funeral parlor. If she continued talking like this, Bryce might accommodatingly kill her so that she could really experience one, she thought.

"I see," Bryce snapped, all his hopes for altering Desha's sense of style flying right out the proverbial window. "Well, do let me know if there's anything else we can do for you," he intoned dryly.

"There is," she hurried to say, thinking she would let him know how dedicated she intended to be. "If I'm to be of any real help, I need to know the inside workings of *Southern Elegance*."

"But, of course," Bryce said in a slightly mocking tone. "Please see to it, Bernice. It's the lady's first day, and she wants to learn everything."

Desha looked at him evenly. "I don't want you to be sorry you hired me, Bryce. An employee needs to know everything she can, to be of maximum benefit."

"Of course," he said, shaking his head as he met her steady gaze. Twenty-three years old, and she thought she had the whole world figured out, he mused. And yet, as irritated as he was with this high-handed peacock of a woman, he had to give her credit: she had confidence! She was so self-assured that he found himself both amused and admiring.

"And, Desha, don't try to set the world on fire with sales your first week. Leave something for the other clerks, all right?"

"Competition is the red blood of free enterprise. As a businessman, you should know that, Bryce."

He had to smile, in spite of himself. He had never heard the term put quite that way. The last he'd heard, it was lifeblood, not red blood.

"Ahh, but remember that I don't want my clerks clamoring to make a sale. I want them to feel they can support themselves on their salary," he told her. "Oh, by the way, Desha, where did you find living accommodations?"

Tilting her head proudly, she told him the name of her hotel. He stroked his chin and smiled at her. "If I remember correctly, that *isn't* on the water, is it?"

"It's where *I* wanted to stay," she told him firmly.

He nodded, and Desha watched as he winked at Bernice, then left the shop. She lifted her chin. She was no idle boaster—she believed she could increase profits at this shop, and she intended to try.

Her astrological guide had indicated new business adventures today, and Desha firmly believed this was it. She saw this as a challenge, as well as a way to repay Bryce for his kindness.

With Bryce's mother's financial backing, Desha really thought she could turn this shop into a real money-maker. All the place needed was some of her Aries fire and flair. She was sure of it. Ideas were already forming. She would think on it and see what the actual situation was here as the week passed.

"Do you know anything about working in a dress shop?" Bernice asked, stirring Desha from her thoughts.

"Yes, I had my own shop in South Carolina." She could see the doubt in Bernice's eyes, but it didn't disturb her. She didn't care if anyone believed her or not. Her finesse would speak for her.

"Fine," Bernice said. "Let me show you around. First and foremost, here's a list of phone numbers that might come in very handy. This one is Bryce's mother's—the shop owner. These are emergency numbers for police and fire."

Desha nodded and followed silently, absorbing information, noting that Bryce's mother was listed as Elayne, then turning her attention elsewhere as Bernice guided her from rack to rack in the store.

When she had seen everything, she asked, "Why doesn't *Southern Elegance* carry a more contemporary line of merchandise?"

Bernice smiled patiently. "*Southern Elegance* is a certain look, a way of life, a Southern way of life. We're very traditional. The owner has always maintained that fads come and go but good taste is ever stylish. It's a matter of pride—Southern pride. Our customers expect to come in here and buy a certain look, a conservative, yet elegant look. That's why they shop here."

"How do you know?" Desha asked, her brow furrowed in thought. She had nothing against a "certain" look. Many women were the height of fashion without varying their wardrobes much from season to season, but even they knew that a new touch, an added accessory, a mixing of old and new, were needed to keep them updated.

Bernice glanced at Mira, then laughed softly. "We know because they come in here instead of going down the street to *Mod Garb*."

Desha nodded thoughtfully. "What manufacturer do you buy from?"

"Come to the office, and I'll show you the inside operation if you're really interested and not just trying to impress the boss," Bernice said.

"I don't have time to play games in my career," Desha said sincerely. "I'm not into that."

Bernice smiled. "I think you really do want to learn, Desha. Well, that's fine with me. I've just returned from a New York buying trip. The new line will arrive the middle of the month. I'll show it to you in the catalog."

"Does the manufacturer stock a mod line?" Desha asked.

"Yes, but of course it isn't of any interest to us. You'll see that our customers don't want the bulging shoulder pads and hemlines almost to their ankles." She glanced at Desha's outfit. "Of course, some people love the fads," she hastened to add, "but not our customers."

Desha's mind was spinning as Bernice led her to a small room located in the back of the building. She wanted to know everything from whether the store had an account number to when the bills arrived. It was typical of her to submerge herself completely in any project, and she was pleased that Bernice was most helpful and direct in supplying information.

By the time the weekend came, Desha felt that she was very familiar with *Southern Elegance*. The clients were mostly locals, and they were wealthy, as Bryce had said. Many had shopped in the store since its inception.

Some were clearly surprised by Desha's appearance, but she went about her business, smiling and assisting politely. She knew clothes, and she was able to help. Soon the regulars turned to her eagerly for advice.

Desha was startled to find Bryce waiting for her in the parking lot when she closed the shop on Friday night. Bernice had given her the keys to the door because Mira had left early.

Bryce leaned across the car seat to open the door of a white Cadillac. "Get in and I'll take you to dinner," he said. "I want to see how your work week went."

He kept his smile firmly in place, but in truth, he knew exactly how Desha's work week had gone. He had called Bernice every day to get a progress report, and he had been glad to learn that, despite Desha's distinct style, the customers liked her and seemed to trust her judgment.

He had been glad, and oddly enough, he admitted, not all that surprised. There was a rare quality about Desha—Bryce couldn't quite label it—a frankness, an indomitable spirit, an openness that was appealing.

He stared at her as she climbed into the Cadillac and turned in the seat so that she could look at him. "This is a surprise," she said. "Do you take all your employees out to dinner at the end of their first week?"

Bryce met her eyes and tried to decide how to answer. He never took his employees anywhere, that is, no one except Juliette who happened to be his stockbroker. "No," he said simply.

When Desha heard his hesitation, she immediately misinterpreted it. "Don't tell me this is another act of charity!" she cried.

Bryce started the car. "No, of course not. I really wanted to see how your week went. After all, you'll be alone in the shop next week. Surely you must realize that I don't usually hire a stranger off the street and give her the keys to one of the family businesses."

Desha settled back against the plush seat. "I should hope not," she admitted. Her dark eyes searched his face. "But then I don't know you. I don't know what you might do."

Bryce chuckled. He didn't know what she might do either, but he had to admit that it intrigued him. He couldn't fathom the reasons for his interest in this woman.

"Don't worry about it until I give you reason to," he teased. "Tonight we're going to get to know each other better. Then you'll know more what to expect from me."

Desha studied him thoughtfully for a moment, her mind racing. Just what did he mean by that? Was he leading up to something? "You do have a girlfriend, don't you?" she asked. "You don't think I'll go out with you just because you hired me to work in the shop, do you?"

Bryce shook his head in disbelief. "You know you really are something. I can't believe your arrogance! Of course I don't expect you to date me because I hired you! This is purely business. Believe me, you're hardly my type, and if you were, let me assure you I wouldn't have to *hire* you to get a date!"

Good heavens, he groaned to himself when he had finished his little tirade. He was beginning to sound like Desha!

Oh no! she had done it again, Desha told herself. Of course he was insulted. Of course he didn't have to hire women to date them. She had phrased that poorly, to say the least. She couldn't believe such a stupid question had come out of her mouth!

She really had wanted to know if he had a girl-friend, and she really had wanted to know what his motives were in hiring her. He had been unusually nice to a stranger. But right now she herself was too insulted to dwell on that point.

"Believe me, you aren't my type either," she cried, wounded to the core. "And just what do you expect me to think when you invite me to dinner, then tell me you don't usually do that with your employees?"

They sat there and glared at each other for a long moment, both locked in their own thoughts. "All I'm asking you to do is have dinner with me, purely business, and only this time," Bryce said at last, trying to gain some control of the situation.

Desha shook her head. "I don't think so. I don't think it's a good idea. You'd better stick with your *type.*"

Bryce opened his mouth in surprise, then closed it as he watched her get out of his car. As soon as she had shut the door, he drove off.

Desha stood on the street and stared after him. She could have had dinner with him, but she realized that she was too disappointed. She *had* thought Bryce was personally interested, and she hadn't been at all opposed to the idea, despite knowing that it was foolish to encourage him.

Aries and Taurus: a ram and a bull. They would be butting heads constantly. But that hadn't been uppermost in her mind when he invited her to dinner. She had just wanted to be sure about his motives. Well, she hoped she had learned her lesson. If she had stuck to business, this wouldn't have happened.

Bryce frowned as he looked back over his shoulder and saw Desha standing on the street. He was more disappointed than he wanted to admit. He *had* been looking forward to getting to know her a little better.

He honestly didn't know why. She was just a crazy stranger who stirred a charitable response in him, wasn't she? A stranger who tended to be most insulting at that!

He stepped on the gas and roared off into the night, but he couldn't block out the picture of Desha standing out on the street in front of stately *Southern Elegance*. The woman and the business defined two contrasting worlds.

Bryce was unaccountably depressed to realize that they pointed out the difference between his and her life. He didn't know why it mattered, he only knew that it did.

Chapter Three

Desha was surprised at how quiet the store was on Saturday. Even she had expected a lot more customers. As she gazed out the window, her mind on the possible ways to increase business, Bernice walked up to her.

"I see that wistful look on your face," the older woman said. "It's spring fever, or more likely beach fever. I had it myself when I was your age."

"Oh, it isn't—" Desha began, but Bernice shook her head.

"Why don't you take the rest of the afternoon off, Desha? Business is unusually slow today, and I don't think anyone will mind if you leave early. Besides, Bryce and his mother are generally much too busy with personal plans to drop by on Saturdays. I'm sure they would understand."

Desha almost politely refused when she thought about Bryce. After all, he had already paid her to

work, but she changed her mind. *Southern Elegance*
just *wasn't* busy enough for both her and Bernice to
work the entire day. She reasoned that she could be
more constructive thinking about how she could increase business. To do that, she needed a quiet place
to ruminate. The beach was just the place for her.

"If you really think it will be all right," Desha said,
"I'd love to go."

Bernice smiled. "Go ahead. That's what being
young in a beach town is all about, isn't it? Ah,
youth," she said playfully.

"But it isn't just for an afternoon of fun in the
sun," Desha said. She caught herself just in time. She
didn't want to tell the other woman her plans.

Bernice looked puzzled. "What is it, then?"

A blush tainted Desha's cheeks. "It's—it's a time to
think, to relax."

Bernice laughed. "Yes, I'm sure it is. Go on. Have
a good time."

An hour later, Desha was sitting on the beach
watching the white-capped waves rush the shore. The
day was windy and there was a lot of water activity.
Wearing a yellow hat to protect her face from sun—
and her nose from freckles—Desha was lost in her own
world as she considered how to best change *Southern
Elegance*'s image. She would have to change its stock.

She was absolutely positive she could increase business by getting a fresh new line in the store. That
didn't mean that the old one had to go, of course, but
there certainly had to be something else to draw the
customers.

Despite Bryce and Bernice's conservative clothing
and attitudes, there were plenty of people, including

the younger set and the fashion trendsetters, who wanted to keep up with the times, South or no South. And, after all, this was a beach city!

Unconsciously, she toyed with the straps of her brief green bikini bathing suit. She had left them down so that her shoulders would tan evenly. She sensed someone's presence and sat up abruptly. To her surprise, Bryce stopped before her, his legs widespread, his arms crossed.

His brow furrowed, he stared down at the woman before him. So, he told himself as his gaze involuntarily swept over her, this was what Desha was hiding beneath the baggy clothes. In her scant attire, she was breathtakingly appealing with high, full breasts, a tiny waist, well-proportioned hips, and pretty legs. He couldn't believe how maddeningly his heart beat at the sight. He had to resist the most absurd urge to draw her up into his arms.

"Bryce!" she cried.

When she spoke, he finally remembered why he had come. "What are you doing here?" he demanded, speaking sharply to cover the excitement she created in him.

Desha tugged at her straps, trying to tie them around her neck so that she wouldn't lose her suit top. Bryce's blue eyes unavoidably strayed to the lightly tanned curves of her breasts visible over the brief top.

Desha had been so happy to see him that she only now realized how harshly he'd spoken. But then what had she expected? They hadn't parted on the most amicable of terms the last time they had seen each other.

"What are *you* doing here?" she retorted, turning the tables on him. "With miles of beach, how did you find me?"

"Bernice told me where you had gone. I walked down the beach until I saw you."

"Oh," Desha said.

"What happened?" he asked, hoping she'd mistake the huskiness of his voice for gruffness. "Was it not in the stars for you to work today?"

Her dark eyes flashed as she looked at him. Poor Bernice, she told herself. Perhaps Bryce had so intimidated the woman that she hadn't confessed that she had given her permission for Desha to leave. Well, it didn't matter. She didn't want to get Bernice in trouble, and she had always fought her own battles. She could have chosen to stay.

"It was ridiculous for me to work with Bernice there. Shucks! There's hardly enough business for one person, much less two."

"But you were hired—and paid—to work today," Bryce returned.

Pursing her lips together, Desha glanced away. She didn't want to tell him that all she'd been thinking about was work—that she was contemplating the best way to increase business. She realized that she didn't want to talk to him about it at all.

When she figured out exactly how she would improve sales, she wanted it to be a big surprise for Bryce. She wanted to *show* how she could help him, not tell. Thus far, she hadn't had much luck putting things into words with this man, and she didn't want to ruin this.

She knew that she hadn't justified his confidence in her yet, but she would. She wanted to see his handsome face light up at her ingenuity. She wanted him to be proud of her, to be glad that he had hired her. She wanted him to have a reason to be nice to her again, instead of glaring at her and snapping at her as he was doing now, instead of judging her and finding her wanting.

Casually scanning the beach, Desha suddenly stopped. She couldn't believe it.

Strolling down the beach in blue jeans, a blue shirt, and sun glasses was the tall, lanky man who had robbed her. Just as if he weren't a criminal! Just as if he had every right to rob her and go on about his business! Well, sun glasses wouldn't hide him from her! Jumping up without a word to Bryce, she raced after the robber.

Bryce stared after her openmouthed. What the devil was she doing now? He couldn't believe his eyes. She was actually running away from him, racing down the beach as if she expected him to do her real harm. Incredulous, he gave chase.

The robber glanced over his shoulder, and when he saw Desha behind him, he began to run, his long legs carrying him farther and farther away.

"Desha! Stop!" Bryce called, attracting everyone's attention. "Damn!" he cursed breathlessly.

Desha glanced over her shoulder, but she didn't have time to explain to Bryce that she couldn't stop. She was not going to let the robber get away this time! When she turned back around, she had lost sight of him.

"Shucks!" she muttered, looking all around. She didn't see him anywhere. How could he have vanished so quickly? So totally? This was all Bryce's fault. If he hadn't called out to her, she wouldn't have turned around, and if she hadn't turned around, she wouldn't have lost the robber.

Abruptly Bryce caught up with her and spun her around. Desha hadn't realized that he was that close behind her. She crashed into him and would have fallen to the ground if he hadn't embraced her.

For a moment, Bryce couldn't let her go. Her beautiful body was pressed to his, from her breasts to her thighs. He could smell that faint perfume she wore. Today the slight lilac smell was mingled with the apple-scented shampoo she'd washed her hair with. His hands were on her skin, and he suddenly ached to trace the curves of her body with his fingertips. Fighting to gain control, he thrust her from him.

"What on earth did you think you were doing?" he asked. "Have you lost your mind? Why were you running from me?"

Breathless, Desha stared at him. "I was chasing the robber! That's what I was doing. If you would have let me alone, I would've caught him too."

"Chasing the robber," he repeated. Then, for what seemed to be an eternity, he stared at her. "I don't believe this," he finally muttered. "I really don't believe it. What did you expect to do with the man if you caught him?"

"Demand that he return my money," she said defiantly. "If I had to, I was prepared to make a citizen's arrest."

"Make a citizen's arrest?" he repeated. His gaze skimmed down her small, shapely body, every curve and line tantalizingly revealed in the skimpy suit. She could hardly force a man to stand still while she arrested him. The whole thing was so ridiculous that Bryce tossed his head back and laughed.

"What's so funny?" she demanded.

"You," Bryce admitted. "You. Do you really think you could get the man to wait while you arrested him?"

"I'll have you know that I've studied jujitsu," she said, drawing herself up proudly.

Bryce shook his head. He should have expected her to come up with something like this. "Then why didn't you use it when the man accosted you?" he asked, barely able to keep a smile off his face.

"He caught me off guard. After all, I didn't expect to be robbed that day. I don't beat up anybody just because he walks up to me, you know."

Bryce shook his head. "Desha, leave the man to the police. You have no business chasing him." His eyes met hers, and he realized that he was very concerned about her. She was behaving recklessly, doing something as foolish as pursuing a robber. Her confident attitude might be appealing, but it could get her into serious trouble.

"You could get hurt," he added softly.

"Don't you worry about me," she insisted. "I can take care of myself. I've been doing so all my life, and things aren't going to change now."

So she could take care of herself, he repeated to himself. And what a stunning job she was doing—moving from state to state, driving a wreck of a car, trying to be an actress, trying to make a go of a clothing store, getting robbed and ending up broke in a new town.

As he looked at her, he had the strongest urge to draw this strange woman into his arms and tell her that he wanted to take care of her, but he shook off the ridiculous thought. That was taking charity too far!

"You really should leave it to the police," he repeated. "You don't know what that man's capable of."

"And he doesn't know what I'm capable of," Desha said. "If he thinks he can rob me and go on about his business, he can think again."

Bryce let his hands slide down Desha's arms. He couldn't help but notice how smooth her skin was. He clasped her fingers in his. "Don't do anything foolish," he said gently. "I don't want to lose my newest employee. You do still work for me, don't you?"

"Yes, of course. I explained about today," she said. "You didn't think that I had taken the advance and then skipped out on you, did you?"

He grinned at her. "No, I suppose not. I know how you feel about charity." He squeezed her fingers, then freed them.

Desha felt her face color, and she didn't know why she was embarrassed. Was it because Bryce had squeezed her fingers . . . or was it because she knew he thought she was trying to cheat him out of a day's pay? She was aware that her heart was beating much too fast. Was that only because she had been running? Surely her heartbeat had slowed by now.

Bryce lingered a moment longer. He realized that he had considered the possibility that Desha had left for good when he went to the shop and found that she wasn't there. He had been very upset—more upset than he had any right or excuse to be. He wanted Desha to keep working for him. He wanted that very much.

"Then you will return to work on Monday, won't you?"

Desha met his eyes. "Of course."

"Good." He studied her face as if he might forget it over the next day. Then, realizing what he was doing, he turned on his heel and walked away.

Desha stared after him until she couldn't see him any longer. She didn't understand the man. If he didn't see her as a charity case and he wasn't interested in her as a woman, what was his interest? Was it all business? Did he want her to work in his shop that badly?

It surely seemed that way. And she made a vow that she wouldn't disappoint him. She was going to make a success of that store, or her name wasn't Desha Deserra. Desha Smith, she corrected herself.

By Monday, Desha had decided on her strategy. Her horoscope had advised that she should make a career move today, and she was sure this was it. She would call the manufacturer, use the account number, and try to have a line of mod clothes added to the delivery that Bernice had said would arrive during the middle of the month.

She got so carried away, once she had made up her mind what to do, that she could concentrate on nothing else. She knew it would work. She just knew it!

All morning, when she wasn't busy, she pored over the catalog Bernice had shown her, trying to decide which styles would be best to start with.

The plan began to take on more and more importance. She had felt since her first day in Virginia Beach that it would be her permanent home, where she made her mark. Obviously succeeding in the shop was in the stars for her, and who could fight fate?

Deciding not to delay a moment longer, she rushed to the phone and dialed the manufacturer's number.

She hung up before it could ring. What was she doing? Bryce had given her blanket permission to increase business, and she did want very badly to impress him—but, after all, this was his mother's store.

She stared at the phone. She had promised herself to think before she acted. Even though this was to help the store, she determined she should talk to *someone* about her plans, and she didn't want it to be Bryce. Besides, he was so stubborn, so set in his ways.

She looked at the list of emergency numbers, picked the phone up again and dialed Elayne's number. When a woman answered on the third ring, Desha asked, "Is this Mrs. Gerrard? Mrs. Elayne Gerrard, Bryce's mother?"

"Yes, this is Mrs. Elayne Gerrard Hammond, Bryce's mother."

"Oh, Mrs. *Hammond*. You've remarried."

"Yes, I have, and who is this?"

Desha heard the distinct curiosity in the other woman's voice. "Desha—Desha Smith. I work for you."

There was a slight pause, then Elayne said, "Of course! Desha. I've heard about you."

"You have?" Desha murmured. "From Bryce? Oh, dear, I hope it wasn't all bad."

There was a hint of amusement in Elayne's voice. "No, not at all. How may I help you, Desha? Is there a problem at the store?"

Desha sighed in relief. This wasn't going to be as bad as she thought. Mrs. Hammond sounded like a much more agreeable person than Bryce. "Well, yes and no," she said, plunging right in.

"Oh?" Elayne sounded puzzled.

"Well, I don't think I need to tell you that business could be better," Desha said, rushing on while her courage still held. "I've had some ideas, and I wondered if I might make a few changes. I can promise you the store will prosper because of them. I'm *sure* of it," she said with conviction.

"Changes in the store? Have you discussed this with Bryce?"

"Well, kind of, but not really," Desha said, faltering. "I—I want it to be a surprise. To tell you the absolute truth, Mrs. Hammond, I want to impress Bryce, to show him what a good businesswoman I am. I don't think he realizes just how good I am in a dress shop. I did have my own in South Carolina."

"You did?" Elayne sounded pensive. There was a lengthy pause before she spoke, and when she did, the amused tone was back in her voice. "Well, why not, Desha? Go ahead and make your changes. Let's see what you can do to increase business."

"Oh, great! Thank you, Mrs. Hammond."

Delighted, Desha disconnected, then immediately went on with her original plans, dialing the manufacturer's number. It seemed the most natural thing in the world since she knew the account number and was familiar with ordering merchandise. Everything went as smooth as silk. *Southern Elegance* was an old and valued customer. If the manufacturer was surprised by this added line, the girl taking the order didn't let on.

When that part of the plan was completed, Desha gazed around the shop, trying to decide how she could best do the redecorating. She was briefly tempted to talk to Bryce about it, but she quickly suppressed that thought. It would spoil the big surprise.

Actually, she decided, all it would really take was a can of orange paint and some yellow flowers. The new line of clothes would do the rest. She would put select items right on the walls, as she had done in her South Carolina store.

She breathed another sigh of relief. This was going much easier than she had anticipated. In fact, it was almost easy to forget that this wasn't her South Carolina store where she was getting a second chance to succeed.

Suddenly she understood something more. She needed to show not only Bryce, but herself, that she could make a success of the shop. The South Carolina flop had been harder on her ego and dreams than she had realized. She was *determined* to make a go of this, and she knew she could.

Now all she needed was a new name—or at the least an amended name for the shop. *Southern Elegance* reminded her of a scene out of a fifties movie. It sounded like an afternoon tea party at Aunt Matilda's mansion, complete with gloves, hats, and snooty social climbers. She sat down on the tan stool behind the counter and began to give it some serious thought.

The days passed rapidly, and Desha's second week at the store ended without undue incident. Friday night after she had locked the door to customers, she puttered around the store, straightening clothes on the racks and making sure the appropriate sizes were placed together. She knew that she was dallying, halfway hoping that Bryce might show up as he had done last Friday night.

She made herself think about Sunday, instead of Bryce. When she locked up tomorrow night, she would close all the blinds, as usual, then Sunday morning, bright and early, she would come with her can of orange paint and redo the store.

A shiver of excitement raced over her at the thought, and she began to concentrate on her redecorating. She was sure that the changes would be pleasing to Mrs. Hammond, and wouldn't Bryce be delighted when he saw what a few orange stripes and stars could do for that plain tan color?

As Bryce dressed on Friday night, he realized that he had deliberately avoided the shop this week. He was too interested in his newest employee, and that would never do. She wasn't his type at all. He had always heard that opposites attracted, but he had never believed it until Desha stumbled into his life.

It really was ridiculous to think of himself becoming involved with her—even if she were interested, which apparently she was not. Cupid couldn't make such an error! It was all wrong. They were all wrong.

Interesting, he mused, that she had said the stars hadn't yet aligned right for her for marriage. He only had one excuse. He just hadn't met the woman who seemed right for what he fully intended to be a lifetime commitment. Marriage was such a serious step.

Suddenly he envisioned Desha in an elaborate satin wedding gown, a garland of white gardenias in her hair. The picture was quite appealing. He shoved it from his mind. What on earth was he thinking of?

He looked at his watch as he finished dressing. He still had time to run by his mother's house before his date with Juliette.

Tonight he drove the white Cadillac, and after he left the beautiful renovated farmhouse on the fifty acres he called home, he went to an exclusive neighborhood and parked in the driveway of Elayne Hammond's sprawling white house.

Desha had implied that *Southern Elegance* wasn't doing well, but it had done well enough to provide Elayne with all the luxuries of life.

His mother answered the door before Bryce had a chance to ring the bell. "Oh, darling, good evening," she said brightly. "I thought you were at the Stanfords'. Come on in and speak to Stephen. He's still getting used to having a stepson."

Bryce laughed. "You're newlyweds. When does he have time to even think about having a stepson?"

Elayne glanced over her shoulder. "You know he's very fond of you, Bryce. He doesn't have any children, and you're our only hope if either of us is ever going to see grandchildren."

"Now, Mother," Bryce chided softly, "don't start."

Undeterred, Elayne asked, "How can I help it? Good heavens, Bryce! I'm sixty-one years old. My knees are going to be too arthritic to bounce grandchildren if you wait much longer to give me some."

"Mother," he cautioned, "we've had this conversation before."

Elayne sighed dramatically. "Yes, we have, haven't we? Well, it is Friday night. Don't you have a date with Juliette?"

"Yes." Abruptly, he changed the subject. "Are you having a dinner party?"

"We decided not to since we're having the pool party on Sunday. Now don't you and Juliette be late. It's going to be a wonderful party, but tonight is only a bridge game."

"Ah, the life of a lady of leisure," he teased. "Aren't you ever going to spend any more time at the shop?"

"At the moment, I'm not quite sure what my plans are where the shops are concerned—"

"What?" Bryce exclaimed, interrupting her. "Surely you're joking! The stores have always been so important to you, especially *Southern Elegance*. And I thought being a homebody bored you."

Elayne laughed softly. "Your father has been dead eight years, Bryce. It was hard to be a homebody alone. Now that I have Stephen, it's fun."

"I see," he said, following her as she moved fluidly in the simple gold caftan she wore. Despite her age lament, she was tall and tan and still very attractive, with graying hair and bright blue eyes.

"The homebody life agrees with you," he complimented. "You're looking exceptionally lovely tonight."

"Oh, you flatterer," she retorted. "Come on out and have a drink with Stephen and me."

"A quick one," Bryce said. "I was late for my last date with Juliette. I don't want that to happen again. She'll think I'm making a habit of it."

Elayne pulled open the sliding glass door. Her eyes met her son's. "Are you?"

"Don't be silly. You know I stopped to help Desha when her car broke down."

"Ah, yes, Desha." Elayne seemed thoughtful. "How's she doing at the shop? You are keeping an eye on her, aren't you?"

"Yes, of course. Bernice is very impressed with her work."

"And you, son, tell me—what do you think of this girl?"

"Desha?"

"Yes, I believe that's who we're talking about."

Bryce smiled suddenly. "You've really got to meet her, Mother."

Elayne smiled. "So I'm told, and believe me, I intend to. I just haven't had time." She didn't mention that she had talked to Desha on the phone.

Bryce walked out onto the magnificent covered patio that surrounded a massive blue pool. There were enough tables and lounge chairs to seat fifty comfortably. The private beach was a mere few feet beyond the end of the pool.

"Is being in love that time-consuming?" he joked.

"Why don't you try it, and see for yourself?" Elayne asked, her eyes meeting his.

Stephen spoke before Bryce could answer. "Good evening, Bryce. What brings you here?"

The younger man smiled and warmly clasped Stephen's hand. He noticed that Stephen, looking as distinguished and polished as ever, wore a masculine version of Elayne's gold caftan.

"One would never know that you two just returned from honeymooning in Egypt," Bryce teased, deliberately assessing the caftan.

"You should try one of these," Stephen returned. "They're so comfortable."

"Sorry," Bryce joked. "I see enough dresses at the shop."

Stephen clapped him on the shoulder and laughed. "What can I fix you to drink?"

"Scotch on the rocks, if you will."

"No date tonight?"

"I'm having dinner with Juliette in half an hour."

"When are you going to give that girl an engagement ring?" Stephen teased. "You don't know what you're missing by not being married." He held out his hand to Elayne, and when she glided into his arms, he kissed her lightly on the lips. "This is the life," he told Bryce, winking at him.

"It seems to be."

Bryce took a sip of his Scotch. He didn't know why he was suddenly feeling very much alone. He liked Stephen, and he was thoroughly delighted that his mother had found love again. She had been lonely for too long. But as he watched the couple embrace, he felt as if a part of his own life was missing.

"I'd better run," he said. "Enjoy your evening."

"You, too," Elayne and Stephen chorused.

"Bring your girlfriend next time," Stephen said. "She's a real looker."

"Yes, she is, isn't she?" Bryce murmured, and he wondered why the woman he saw in his mind's eye was Desha. This time she wore the brief green bikini, but she looked as outrageous as ever as he remembered her running down the beach in that yellow hat. He smiled a little to himself—the woman was as outrageous as she looked.

Impulsively, he decided to go by the shop and make sure that it was locked up. He dared not let himself think that what he really wanted was to see Desha. He had deliberately stayed away from her all week. Besides, surely she had already left for the evening.

Desha looked at her big-faced wristwatch and frowned. There was no point in delaying going home any longer. Bryce wasn't coming. It was way past closing time. She was annoyed with herself for feeling so disappointed. She hadn't seen the man all week, and she realized that she had hoped every single day that he would come into the shop to see how she was doing.

Sighing, she got her carpetbag from behind the counter and walked to the door. She peered out through the blinds, thinking perhaps that Bryce had parked in the side parking lot where she couldn't see him. But his car wasn't there. No one's was.

It was useless to procrastinate. When she had closed the door behind her, she locked it. Then she looked both ways and slowly began to walk down the street. Tonight she didn't relish the idea of going to her hotel room all alone. She hadn't yet made any friends. Most of the people there were tourists—mainly families— making the most of their vacation by spending all their time on the beach. They weren't there to make new friends.

When a car pulled up beside Desha, she was so startled that she jumped. Bryce lowered the window.

"Want a ride home?" he asked as his eyes swept over her outfit. She was dressed as uninhibitedly as ever tonight, in more pinks and lavenders, an artificial rose hibiscus in her short hair.

Still, she hadn't neglected her earrings. Her ears were accented with bright pink blossoms. She was colorful, but as Bryce looked at her, he couldn't help but find her delightful in some exotic way, like the most brilliant flower in the garden.

Trying to hide her excitement, Desha pulled open the door and climbed in. "Hello, Bryce. What are you doing here this time of night?"

He shrugged. "I thought I'd be sure the shop was securely locked." He smiled at her. "Not that I don't trust you to lock up. It's an old habit of mine from all the years Mother ran the shop."

"She actually worked at the shop?" Desha asked, surprised. She let her gaze skim down Bryce's expensive gray suit and blue shirt. He looked more handsome than usual.

"She worked at the shop for more than forty years, the last eight as owner. She loved it. She's very people-oriented."

"Me, too," Desha said. "Aries people are naturally extroverted. I get along with everybody."

Bryce smiled. Because she was so flamboyant and outspoken, it seemed a contradiction, but apparently she did get along well with people. "I'm sure you do."

"Listen, Bryce," she said, suddenly inspired, "you know that dinner you invited me to last week? Well, I'll take you up on that tonight."

That wasn't quite the way she had meant to bring up the subject, but it was done now. She was alarmed by the intense beating of her heart. She really wanted him to say yes, and she was very much afraid he wouldn't.

She told herself that she wouldn't care so much if she hadn't realized a short time ago how lonely she was, but on the other hand, she hadn't realized she was lonely until she had decided that Bryce wasn't coming by the shop. Now that he had, she really wanted to spend more time with him.

He pulled up into the hotel parking lot. "I'd really like to—"

"Oh, great! Can you give me a minute to change into something else? You look so sharp." She was already reaching for the door handle.

"Desha!"

His tone stopped her. "You didn't let me finish," he said softly. "I already have plans for tonight."

She felt a blush rise up her neck to her cheeks. "Well, why didn't you say so?"

"I'm sorry. I tried." He truly was sorry. She looked so disappointed that he wanted to go with her.

"Well, why did you give me a ride home if you had other plans?" she asked, speaking crossly to cover her eagerness and embarrassment.

He smiled faintly. "I told you I stopped by to make sure the shop was locked. I saw you on the street and, since I was going this way, I thought I would save you the walk." It was the same lie he had told himself and it sounded even less believable the second time.

"Don't bother next time," she said, reaching for the door handle again. She couldn't recall the last time she had been so embarrassed. But then she didn't usually go around asking a man out for the evening, even in these enlightened days.

Bryce grasped her shoulder and made her face him. "Next time," he said, "we'll have dinner."

Her dark eyes met his. Before he thought about what he was doing, he drew her to him and his lips lightly brushed hers.

When he freed her, he murmured, "All right?"

Her pulse racing, her mouth suddenly very dry, she nodded. "All right."

Then she reached for the door handle and climbed out. As she stood on the sidewalk and watched Bryce drive away, she wanted desperately to know where he was going. Did he have a girlfriend? She had asked him before, but he hadn't answered.

She wanted very much to have dinner with him. But she wanted him to kiss her again even more. Holding her fingers to her lips, she went into her hotel.

Chapter Four

On Sunday morning, Desha was up with the sun, eager to enhance the color in *Southern Elegance*. Redoing the shop had taken on even more importance when Bryce brushed her lips with his.

She was set on showing him that she could help him prosper, although she wasn't entirely sure why that should matter so much to her. Suddenly it had become more than just a matter of repaying Bryce for what he had done for her. She very much wanted him to think highly of her.

Dressed in green coveralls, a red bandana wrapped around her head, and tennis shoes on her feet, she opened the can of orange paint and set about implementing her plans. Masking tape outlined the areas she intended to color bright orange.

On one wall, she had marked off four huge stripes. On another, she had marked off three massive stars, as well as three smaller stars on each of the dressing room doors. On the third wall, she had combined stars and stripes, and on the fourth, she had marked off a square that grew progressively larger until it covered the whole wall, making an optical illusion that gave the wall a sense of depth.

Before she began her work, she turned on the radio, changing the station from one of big band music to fifties' rock and roll. Bouncing along to the beat, she happily set about her work.

By midmorning, she was already through with her painting. She pulled the masking tape off and stood back to survey her handiwork. It looked wonderful.

"Desha Smith," she told herself, "girl, you do have a talent!"

Now the once-dull room fairly bustled with motion and excitement. The bold orange paint made the entire room come alive with sensation and color. The stars and stripes made a dramatic statement; the square beckoned with mysterious illusion.

Desha climbed up on the tan stool and nodded her head. Yes, indeed, with one can of paint, she had made a miracle. Tomorrow was delivery day for the clothing. She prayed that her mod line would arrive with the regular shipment. The paint looked fantastic, but the remodeling would be only half-done until she put her clothes up on the walls in the eye-catching spaces.

Her heart happy, she surveyed the room again, then left the stool to gather up her supplies and clean her paint brush. She could hardly wait for tomorrow morning. She hoped the manufacturer wouldn't disappoint her. She was frantic to show Bryce the store; she was fairly bursting with excitement over his anticipated reaction.

* * *

On Monday, Desha was at the store at eight in the morning. She wanted to be sure that her orange paint was still there and still looked as good as on the day she did it. To her pleasure, it looked even better. She sat around and daydreamed about the rest of her remodeling until it was time to open the doors to customers.

The orange paint certainly generated a lot of excitement, with the square getting the most attention. Desha couldn't tell if the customers liked the new paint or not, but it definitely caught their interest.

All morning, she waited on pins and needles until the big truck pulled up in the parking lot. Anxiously, she spoke to the driver, who was new, and watched as he delivered the stock.

"Wonderful!" she cried, when he started bringing in her contemporary line. The clothes looked terrific—bright and snappy and bold.

The man grinned at her enthusiasm. "It's good to see the customer so happy," he said.

"Oh, this is marvelous!" Desha cried. "I've been waiting for these clothes all morning." She gestured toward the room she had painted. "I'm redecorating."

He peeked around the door and his smile broadened. "Colorful with all that orange, isn't it? And that psychedelic square is a real trip."

Desha frowned slightly. She didn't think of her square as psychedelic. She didn't know Mrs. Hammond—the woman had seemed very nice on the phone—but if she was anything at all like her straight-laced son, she would probably have a stroke if she knew anyone thought anything in her store looked psychedelic.

Suddenly Desha had a terrible thought: what if she had overdone the changes? She tried to push the troublesome notion from her mind. She was planning to put a green and orange jacket right in the middle anyway. Boy, would that be an eye-catcher!

The driver handed Desha the bill to sign, and when she had done so, he sauntered back out the delivery entrance to his truck. "Have a good day," he called over his shoulder.

"Thanks," Desha replied.

She intended to have a good one. She put the new line in the center of the store, between the rows of sophisticated, traditional, sedate clothes. The bright colors gave even the old stock a new life.

Satisfied, her heart beating excitedly, Desha dragged out a huge green poster board she had done in the hotel room. It was a sign with bold orange letters stating the new name of the store: *Southern Elegance & not so elegants*. She placed it right in the front window, then set about finishing her displays.

The orange and green jacket was stunning in the square. Anyone who missed it would have to be blind. A yellow skirt and blouse were tacked in two of the orange stars, while a green dress occupied the other. Two yellow flowers nestled on the dress collar. The stripes were the recipients of assorted clothing, from baggy blouses and cropped pants to skimpy bathing suits. After all, this was the beach!

Desha turned on her tall stool when she heard the bells she had attached to the door jingle. Customers! Well, she was almost finished.

"Oh, Mama, I don't want to shop in this old store," a teenage girl complained. "Why don't you just come to *Mod Garb* and pick me up when you're finished here?" Suddenly she stopped talking and looked around the shop. "Awesome!" she cried. "Truly awesome!"

Desha grinned and finished her display. That girl was one customer *Mod Garb* wasn't going to get. She couldn't deny the sense of relief that flooded through her. Ever since the delivery man's comment, she had felt a little unsure about what she'd done.

Seconds later, she climbed down and went over to the teenager. "Can I help you with anything?"

"Oh, wow, can you ever!" she cried, her gaze sweeping over Desha's contemporary outfit. "I want that orange and green outfit—the one in the stars." She pointed, then turned to the square. "And that jacket!"

Desha glanced at the girl's mother to see her reaction. "Sell her whatever she wants," the woman said with a slight smile. "I'm so happy she's found clothes she likes here. How clever of you to offer something so new along with something so traditional. Now you've made both of us happy, and I won't have to look all over the beach for clothes for my daughter."

Desha grinned proudly and stood straighter, her confidence restored. The shop was going to be a big success. She felt it.

When the mother and daughter left, the till was richer by several hundred dollars. Desha could barely contain her excitement as the next customers walked in. They were two middle-aged women who seemed mildly startled by the shop's new face, but one did mention that she was going to bring her niece with her the next time she came.

A swarm of teenagers passed the open door and one glanced inside as they sauntered by. "Whoa!" she cried to the group. "Look at *Southern Elegance*. It's got righteous clothes on the walls!"

Amid giggles and twitters, the girls rushed inside. Desha beamed as they requested copies of the bathing suits she had put on display. Clearly they were locals, and that was the trade she most wanted to attract because they were year-round customers.

The bells jangled again, and Desha smiled confidently at the people coming into the shop. She was on a natural high. There was no way she could fail now. She felt success in her very bones.

Her smile faded as Bryce plunged into the store, an older, attractive gray-haired lady in his wake.

"What's the meaning of that sign in the window?" he demanded. "Just who gave you permission to change the name—" His words trailed off midway, and he and the woman sucked in their breath at the same time.

"Good heavens!" Bryce muttered, spinning so that he could see all the changes in *Southern Elegance*. He focused on the orange square and stood transfixed before it. Mesmerized, he gazed at it for several seconds.

When he turned away to look at her, Desha's heart began to pound ominously. He didn't seem at all pleased. This wasn't the reaction she had expected. The whole room seemed to stand still while Bryce made his way toward her, his blue eyes blazing, his jaw muscle twitching. Desha's heartbeat echoed in her chest like a jungle drum.

She no longer had a good, successful feeling. This was a man who was angry, and he was coming in her direction. The fifties' music faded; the teenage voices were suddenly mute. The hair on her neck stood on end. Bryce looked like he was ready to strangle her.

Desha quickly looked at the woman who had come in with him, wondering if she would get any help from her. The woman's resemblance to Bryce was so strong that Desha guessed it was Mrs. Hammond herself.

And she seemed literally transfixed by the difference in *Southern Elegance*. She didn't move a muscle. She just stood in one spot, staring. She wasn't going to be a bit of help, Desha thought despairingly—and she had given Desha the go-ahead. Still, clearly neither the woman nor Bryce had anticipated *such* changes, Desha noted unhappily.

She dug in her heels and waited for the onslaught of Bryce's fury. He wasn't even going to listen to what she had to say. Obviously he didn't even see the teenage girls, and he couldn't know how much money the store had already made today. He had seen what he wanted to see—or didn't want to see—as the case may be, and now he was out for blood, her blood!

Alarmed and hurt, she crossed her arms and waited. The wait was brief though it seemed to take Bryce a long time to reach her.

He took her by one wrist and drew her toward him. "Look at this!" he said, pointing to the orange square. "What have you done here? How dare you take such liberties in this shop? I give you an inch, and you take a mile! Don't you have any respect for anyone else's property and rights?"

Crushed, Desha stared forlornly at him. She hadn't thought of what she'd done at all in the way he had.

He didn't understand that she was honestly trying to repay him, not anger and upset him. She had been attempting to make him proud of her. Now she had made the situation even worse.

And maybe she had been out of line. It *did* sound as if she had stepped out of bounds the way Bryce phrased it. Maybe she had gotten so caught up in her own creation that she had acted much too hastily.

"I'm sorry," she murmured. "I didn't think—"

"That's right," he agreed, interrupting her. "You didn't think, period! You just charged right ahead as if you *owned* the shop. You didn't succeed with yours, and now you come here—"

Desha was aware that the teenage girls were no longer talking at all, muted or otherwise. "Bryce," she whispered, "I can explain, really I can if you just wait until the customers are gone."

"You'll explain right now!" he insisted. "Where did you get that line of punky clothes?"

"They're mod, not punk," she declared. The man didn't know one from the other. What was the point in trying to explain what she had done to someone like him? Couldn't he *see* that she had *already* begun to succeed here? He wouldn't even listen to her apology, let alone see what an improvement she had made.

"And I ordered the clothes from the manufacturer. Where do you think I got them?"

"You did what?" he asked, his fingers tightening on her arm. "I don't believe this."

"Let go of me, or I promise you, you'll be sorry," she whispered, her patience suddenly at end.

"Not as sorry as *you'll* be," he warned.

Before either of them could do anything rash, Bryce's mother walked up. She closed her own fingers around Bryce's wrist and drew his hand away. There was a big smile on her face when she looked at Desha.

"So," she said, her voice warm and amused, "you're my new shop clerk." She gazed slowly around the room. "My, my, but you do have your own way of doing things, don't you?"

"She can just stay after work and undo this mess, too," Bryce said, his eyes still blazing when he looked at Desha.

The woman raised her brows. "I don't think so. It *is* a surprise, but I rather like it."

Desha hadn't realized that she was holding her breath until it escaped from her lips in a relieved sigh. "You do?" she murmured. Then she grinned. "Of course you do," she added, trying to reclaim a scrap of the confidence she'd had before Bryce took her to task. At least his mother was appreciative of the time and effort put into improving the store. "Already business is increasing," she added proudly.

She glanced at the teenage girls who were still in the shop, looking expectantly toward the three adults. "Girls," she said brightly, "may I be of any help?"

They seemed reluctant to see the promising fight end, but finally one held up a blue swimsuit. "I need a ten in this. Do you have one?"

Desha marched past Bryce, her long skirt swishing against her legs as she walked. Deliberately ignoring him, she went to the middle of the room and deftly found the size the girl wanted. When she returned, Bryce and the woman were talking in low voices.

"So," Desha said, regaining some of her control because of the woman's approval, "you must be Mrs.

Hammond." She held out her hand, and Elayne clasped it firmly.

"Excuse me. I seem to have forgotten my manners. I'm Elayne Gerrard Hammond, Bryce's mother. And you're Desha. What a refreshing surprise." She slowly studied the room. "Ah, the enthusiasm of youth. I had forgotten with what new eyes the young see things. You do have a certain flourish and flair, my dear."

"You aren't going to leave the shop like this, are you, Mother?" Bryce asked incredulously. "I can assure you I had nothing to do with it. Desha did not have my permission."

"That's not exactly the truth, Bryce Gerrard!" Desha cried. She shook her index finger at him. "You didn't know how I would do it, but you did give your consent for me to increase business."

"Come now, Desha," Bryce muttered, "you didn't think I meant *this*!" He looked around the room. "I had no idea that you would take me seriously, and if I had, I never would have—"

"You never would have what?" Desha asked tightly, her hands on her hips. "I might have 'taken liberties' here, but at least *I* worked in good faith."

"It's all right," Elayne said, her eyes dancing as she watched the interplay between the couple. "*I* gave Desha permission to make some changes in the store. Granted," she said with a laugh, "I had no idea what changes—"

"You did what?" Bryce said. "*You* gave her permission?"

"Yes. She called to ask, and she and I had a nice little chat." She waved a hand at her indignant son. "And, yes, Bryce, of course I'm going to leave the shop this way. Desha has gone to some trouble to re-decorate, and I love the vibrancy!''

She seemed thoughtful for a moment. ''Clerking in this store was the first job I ever had. When I started working here as a young bride, I was in love and full of my own happiness. I wanted to sing to the world, I wanted to make a statement, I wanted to splash color everywhere. Of course I didn't own the shop—'' she looked at Desha ''—and I didn't have the confidence you have, so I just daydreamed about all the things I wanted to do.''

Her eyes met Bryce's. ''It wasn't until you bought the shop for me eight years ago, Bryce, that I could do what I wanted. Remember how carried away I got af-ter all those years of plans?'' She seemed pensive for a moment. ''I don't know when I went to this dull tan.''

''Exactly!'' Desha said. ''The first time I saw it, I thought that it looked like a funeral—'' Her voice trailed off as she recalled what she had thought it looked like. She was going to have to put her tongue in a coffin and bury it yet.

''Desha!'' Bryce muttered beneath his breath, ''Mother did decorate the shop herself.''

Elayne chuckled. ''Leave the girl alone, Bryce. Fu-neral home you were going to say, Desha?''

Unconsciously chewing on her lip, Desha nodded.

''You're so refreshingly honest,'' Elayne said with a chuckle. ''You know, Bryce, she's right. The truth is that the place had no life. And just look at it now!''

Bryce shook his head. He had seen enough. He couldn't believe that his mother was pleased. The place was positively outrageous. Like Desha, he thought, glancing at the woman dressed in a colorful orange-striped skirt and baggy white blouse captured at the waist by a green belt. His gaze lingered on her a moment.

But hadn't he rather grown used to her exotic look? Maybe that would happen with the shop. He looked around it again. Yes, indeed, it was certainly colorful.

"Maybe we should have her redecorate the other shop in town," Elayne said. "What do you think, Bryce?"

"I think we should wait and see what happens here," he replied, dampening Desha's rising excitement. "Let's see if new decor really stirs the customers."

Desha tried not to let her disappointment show. "I don't have any way to get to the other shop right now anyway," she commented, saying the first thing that came to mind.

Elayne turned back to her. "What do you mean?"

"Well, Betty's out of commission and I can't afford—I can't—I don't—" She sighed. She didn't want to tell this woman that she was broke.

Elayne frowned. "Betty?"

Bryce rolled his eyes heavenward. He didn't even want to know who Betty was.

"My car," Desha explained. "Bryce has kindly given me advances," she said tightly, casting her gaze at him, "but my hotel rent is high and I haven't quite gotten back on my feet yet after the robbery."

"Robbery?"

Bryce braced himself, waiting for the lively tale that was sure to come. He wasn't disappointed.

"So you see," Desha said, wrapping up after a detailed recitation of both her and the robber's exploits, with the robber somehow getting the worst of it, "it will take me a little time to get my finances in order. But I'll do it. I'm an Aries."

Elayne was thoroughly sympathetic. "Bryce, have Betty towed to the shop and get Wayne to repair her. We can't have Desha without transportation."

"No, of course not," Bryce said with a trace of mockery.

"Thanks, but no thanks," Desha said, glancing sharply at Bryce. "I've had enough help from you. I'll get Betty repaired when I can afford to."

"See, Mother," Bryce noted. "You just can't be nice to her. I don't know why anyone tries."

"Now listen here—" Desha began, but Elayne broke in.

"I respect your wishes to pay your own way," Elayne said, "but we could consider it a loan."

Desha managed a smile for Elayne. "I really do appreciate it, but no thank you. It sounds more like charity to me, and I can't accept."

Elayne shrugged and raised her brows. "As you wish. Bryce," she said, turning to her son, "I think Desha deserves all the help she can get after she's gone to such trouble here in the shop. Let the city know we've added a new line here at *Southern Elegance & not so elegants*."

Giving his mother a brusque nod, Bryce pressed his lips together in a firm line. He would not say what was on his mind. He would not remind his mother that she had always taken the understated way, preferring sales by word of mouth to advertising.

Elayne smiled at Desha. "I'm having a pool party on Sunday. You must come and meet my new husband and my friends."

Bryce stared at the woman in surprise. Elayne had had a tight circle of friends for years. He couldn't believe she was inviting Desha into that crowd.

"I'll have Norm, my chauffeur, come around to pick you up at two. Where are you staying?"

When Desha gave the name of the hotel, Elayne glanced disapprovingly at Bryce. He looked away. He didn't believe any of this.

"See you on Sunday then," Elayne said. "Ready, Bryce?"

He nodded and walked with her from the shop.

Only after the door closed behind the couple did Desha release her breath in a ragged sigh and admit to herself just how disappointed she really was by Bryce's reaction. Oh, it helped that his mother was pleased, but it had been Bryce she had wanted to impress.

Even if she had perhaps acted presumptuously—and after all, she had only painted a little and ordered one line of clothes—she had done it to help the business! Obviously, it hadn't done *her* all that much good. It certainly hadn't done one whit to make Bryce think more highly of her. And that hurt most of all.

She became pensive, recalling that Elayne said Bryce had bought the shop for her. She hadn't expected that. She wondered where Bryce had got his wealth. Distracted, she went to the counter to take the teenage girls' money for seven bathing suits.

Out on the street, Bryce faced his mother. "Why didn't you tell Desha how you must have really felt about her changes?"

She frowned at him. "I decided I liked them. Didn't you?"

He seemed taken aback, then smiled slightly. "To tell you the truth, I was so shocked that I don't know if I liked them or not."

"But you like Desha," Elayne said.

"Oh, come on, Mother, don't start," he insisted.

"Admit it," she said. "You got too upset not to be emotionally involved with her already. I could tell."

Bryce frowned. Was he that transparent? He was emotionally involved with Desha, but his reaction to the woman paralleled his reaction to the shop. It was so shocking and unexpected that he truly didn't know how he felt about her.

He thought of how, only days ago, he had touched Desha's sweet mouth with his lips. He recalled how good she had felt when she had fallen against him at the beach.

She had stirred something deep within him. He had been alarmed because the reaction was so intense. And he had felt foolish. He had gone home with the firm conviction that he wouldn't see her again, despite the promise of dinner. Now he didn't know what to think.

"I like her, Bryce," Elayne said. "She has spirit and conviction. She thought the shop needed a change, and she gave it one."

"After working there so short a time—and without anyone's *knowledgeable* consent," Bryce pointed out. "If the new line doesn't sell, we're the ones who lose money."

Elayne laughed. "We can afford it, and tell me the truth, would you have knowingly given her permission, Bryce?"

He laughed. "No, of course not."

Elayne smiled. "If she had told me what she had in mind, I would have thought she was crazy. But I really think she will increase our business. She was willing to take a chance—a risk—to increase our business. She's incredibly invigorating. I adored her right away."

Bryce grinned. "She tells me she makes friends easily and that she gets along with everyone. I think you're proving her point. She sure won you over easily enough."

Elayne locked her arm in his as they walked to his car. "Yes, she did. Maybe she'll win you over." She squeezed his arm. "Maybe you'll fall in love with her. I'd sure love to have some grandchildren with all that spirit and new blood. Juliette is so dry."

"Mother," Bryce said sternly.

Elayne met his eyes. "Well, she is, Bryce, and you know it. I believe in ambition, but that woman is a walking investment brochure. Besides, if you really wanted to marry her, I think you would have done it long ago. You've been dating her for years. With Desha, there's new hope!"

Bryce exhaled tiredly. "Mother, don't be ridiculous. Desha and I are as different as night and day, or haven't you noticed?"

"No," she said. "I haven't. You're looking at the wrappings, not the person."

"How can I avoid it? You see the way she dresses, the way she behaves. She's so—so *expressive*!"

"Oh, Bryce, don't be so rigid. She's only doing what untold numbers of other young women do, she's following fashion. That's what makes the clothing industry, my boy, in case you've missed the point. Thank God we don't all dress the same way!"

"It's not just the clothes, Mother. She's out in left field in everything she does. She even consults an as-

trologer, for heaven's sake. She relies on her horoscope for her day's activities.''

Elayne grinned. "How fascinating. I've always been
intrigued by that kind of thing. I wonder if there is any
truth to it.''

"Mother," he said between his teeth, thoroughly
exasperated, "the stars don't control our destiny.''

Elayne laughed. "How do you know? Personally, I
think your fate is already determined. And I think it
has something to do with Desha, and believe me, my
son, if Cupid shoots you with his arrow, even you
won't be able to escape, no matter how you try to reason your way out of it.''

"I swear, Mother, I'm beginning to think you're as
mad as Desha is!''

Elayne laughed. "Maybe it's contagious. Maybe
you'll catch it.''

"No way," Bryce said as he opened the car door for
her. But, in truth, he was afraid he had already caught
it. Whatever it was.

Chapter Five

On Tuesday morning, Bernice came to the shop. She opened the door and gazed around incredulously.

"Hello, Bernice," Desha said cheerfully. "How are you today?"

Bernice grinned as she surveyed the room. "I never would have believed this if I hadn't seen it with my own eyes," she declared good-naturedly. "So, the old order tumbles."

"Oh, no! This is just a blending of the times," Desha said.

"I sure never thought I'd see the day, but Mrs. Hammond seems quite enthusiastic about it." She grinned at Desha. "I hope you pull it off."

"Well, thank you, Bernice."

"In fact, Mrs. Hammond sent me over to help you with the advertising she wants."

Desha frowned. She was eager for a chance to talk to Bryce. She wanted to find out if he was still mad at her. She couldn't get him out of her mind. She realized that she had been hoping he would help with the advertising. It had been a silly thought, of course. Bernice had always worked with her.

"My horoscope says that I'm very creative today," Desha said contemplatively. She glanced around the room. "You know what, Bernice, I'm going to try to combine some of the new with the old." She snapped her fingers. "As I said, a blending of the times. I think it will work! Please come help me put some combinations together."

Clearly Bernice was aghast at the very notion, but she dutifully followed the animated Desha to the traditional racks.

By the time the day ended, sophisticated, sedate brown silk had been enriched with Desha's own brand of style. Huge stretchy orange belts and baggy orange jackets made an evening ensemble; larger-sized sleeveless designer vests with a sleek, dressy look complemented voluminous blouses and long mod skirts, and gave a certain dash of elegance to skimpy bathing suits; wide-shouldered black leather jackets were matched with traditional white jumpsuits. Almost everything in the shop had an unfamiliar complement.

"What do you think?" Desha asked Bernice.

Bernice could only shake her head in wonder. "I'm so impressed," she announced, "that I'm buying two of the outfits myself."

"Good."

When Bernice had purchased her two outfits, helped with advertising, and left the store, Desha gave her attention to several customers who had come in.

Things were shaping up already. If only Bryce would stop by....

The work week went by in a flash for Desha. She tried not to be disappointed because she heard nothing more from Bryce. She still wanted to talk to him, but as the days passed, she had no choice but to turn her total concentration to business.

On Friday night, however, she lingered once again at the store, hoping to see Bryce. She told herself she only wanted to talk to him about his unfair reaction to her shop changes, but in her heart she knew that wasn't the only reason. No matter how hard she tried, she couldn't forget that tiny little kiss he had given her. She couldn't forget those blazing blue eyes. She couldn't forget Bryce.

She definitely felt that he owed her an apology for his behavior. However, she was willing to settle for his admittance that she had done her best to help business. After that unfortunate situation was cleared up, Desha wanted to get on a better footing with Bryce. The truth of the matter was that she was really attracted to him, no matter how unwisely.

She stayed at the shop long after she had closed it, but Bryce didn't come. She tried to hide her disappointment under a cloud of anger, telling herself that he didn't have the nerve to face her, but she was disappointed all the same. Although she fully expected to see him on Sunday at his mother's pool party, she had wanted to get the unpleasant confrontation over before then. Unhappy, she had no choice but to return to her hotel room.

* * *

When Desha read the Sunday paper, she discovered that her horoscope predicted romance for the day. Frowning, she wondered if a new man was on the horizon for her. Yet every time she tried to imagine one, she could only see Bryce Gerrard's face—his piercing blue eyes, black brows and black hair, his tantalizing lips. She trusted her horoscope, but she didn't know what to make of the prediction.

Finally, she devoted her time to trying to decide what to wear to the pool party. She would wear a bathing suit, of course, but which one? And what shoes? Which earrings?

She decided to postpone the decision until after she'd gone out for her breakfast. As she lingered over coffee, the correct choice came to her.

She would wear one of her new, very successful combinations from the shop—a yellow one-piece suit and an oversized brown thigh-length slinky vest. She had a wraparound skirt with alternate bands of brown and yellow that would be perfect with the vest and suit. She would wear yellow earrings and some brown beads. She could complement the outfit with brown high-heeled sandals, and a wide stretchy brown belt.

Satisfied, she went back to her room. When the chauffeur knocked on her door, she was ready. She knew she'd made the right choice in clothing because the chauffeur couldn't seem to stop staring at her.

"Miss Smith?" he asked, trying to keep his gaze steady on her face, and failing.

"Yes. You're Norman?"

He grinned. "That's me. I believe you're going to the pool party at the Hammond's."

She nodded.

He seemed to have something else he wanted to say, but instead, he led the way to a black limousine in the hotel parking lot.

"What a nice car!" Desha exclaimed.

"Nothing but the best for Mrs. Hammond," Norman said, as he opened the back door for Desha.

She ignored him and climbed into the front seat. She didn't see him shake his head as he went around to the driver's side.

"I'm a little nervous about this party," Desha said, chattering away as though she'd known the man forever. "Are there many people coming?"

"About thirty is the usual number."

"I hope they have a big pool," Desha said.

Norman grinned at her. "They have a very big pool."

She looked down at her short skirt and wondered if she should have worn a different outfit. Perhaps she shouldn't have worn her suit at all. Maybe they didn't swim right away at a pool party like the Hammonds were giving. She shrugged off the nagging doubt. A pool party was a pool party. What was the point in having a pool party if no one was going to dress for swimming?

A short time later, she drew in her breath as Norman stopped in front of a sprawling white mansion. "Is this it?" she asked.

He nodded. "This is the place. I hope you'll have a good time, Miss." He started to get out to open the door, but she opened it herself.

"Thanks, Norman. See you later."

He didn't say anything as she walked up to the front door and rang the bell, but he was shaking his head again.

Elayne herself opened the door. Desha's heart sank when she saw that the woman was dressed in a chic silver caftan, silver and gold sandals on her feet. She was the epitome of casual class.

"Desha! How adorable you look!" Elayne exclaimed. "Isn't that one of the designer vests from the shop?"

Desha nodded. "The bathing suit is from the shop, too."

Elayne laughed. "I love the combination. I never would have dreamed of putting the swimsuit and vest together, especially with that skirt, and believe it or not, I once considered myself adventurous in fashion."

Desha smiled, very pleased. "Thank you."

"Well, come in, honey. Most of the others are already out in back."

"You look very lovely," Desha said.

"Why, thank you, dear." She winked at the younger woman. "I got this caftan in Egypt on my honeymoon a couple of weeks ago." She grew thoughtful. "Hmm, do you think that perhaps we should carry them in the shop?"

"I think that's a great idea!" Desha cried. "You know they would be wonderful over bathing suits, and, belted, they would be grand for evening wear."

Elayne smiled. "I love your enthusiasm, Desha, and I'm glad you approve. I'll place an order tomorrow."

Beaming happily, Desha followed Elayne through the lovely house to the patio. It was like something out of a fairy tale. The tables all around the pool were decorated as formally as any Desha had seen in restaurants, with lovely dishes and stiff white napkins. The pool glistened with sparkling blue water.

Her smile faded when she saw the others gathered under the shaded sun deck roof. No one wore a bathing suit. No one except her.

Everyone else was dressed as Elayne was—in caftans, fancy sundresses, long, white Mexican dresses with detailed lace accents, and incredibly dressy sunsuits. The men almost all wore assorted styles of white slacks and Hawaiian shirts. They looked as if they were in uniform. Even Bryce's outfit varied little from the others.

Desha spotted him almost immediately. In his white slacks and understated navy shirt, he had obviously tried for a casual look, but the look was so deliberate that it seemed almost formal.

And he was sitting beside the most gorgeous woman Desha believed she had ever seen. The blonde was dressed in clothing that looked as if it came from *Southern Elegance*, and she lived up to every word of traditional elegance in a soft blue sleeveless floor-length dress. While Desha watched, the blonde patted Bryce's cheek and laughed up at him.

Desha forgot all about her own outfit. Bryce was with that woman! He did have a girlfriend! Her throat began to tighten, and she fought a ridiculous urge to break into tears. She felt as if someone had tricked her. She realized that she'd come here expecting to spend time with him, and he was with someone else!

Battling to regain her composure, lest she embarrass herself, she told herself that she didn't care. After all, what did the blonde have that she didn't? Nothing, except maybe Bryce, she conceded. And that was what mattered most of all.

Desha met his eyes briefly before Elayne started introducing her to the guests. She saw the way his gaze roved over her outfit, and she straightened her spine. Someone should have told her that the rich had the pool only for looks at their pool parties.

Well, she didn't care what Bryce thought of her or her clothes! She had dressed appropriately, and she was going to have a good time. She would even swim in that huge pool if she took a notion to.

Bryce couldn't seem to look away from Desha. She was the most appealing woman present. Every man on the patio was staring at her. Oh, part of it was her costume, of course—it wasn't every day that this group saw such a shapely young woman in such a colorful outfit—but other than that, Desha didn't look so unusual today. He rather liked the short skirt and that long vest with the yellow bathing suit peeking through. He rather liked the woman, and that was the whole problem.

He realized with a jolt that his mother was right. He was emotionally involved with Desha. He had forgotten all about Juliette sitting at his side when Desha walked in. All he had done was kiss the younger woman's lips briefly, but that had been enough, he realized, to make him want so much more.

"Stephen, this is Desha, *Southern Elegance & not so elegants*' newest clerk," Elayne said.

Stephen extended his hand and boldly assessed Desha. "Well, aren't you a pretty little thing? And so young! I've heard a lot about you."

Desha could feel the color rush to her cheeks. "I suppose most of it was bad." Involuntarily, she glanced at Bryce.

"No, it was all good," Stephen insisted. "I understand you're going to make us all richer. I've always thought that's what the rich need—more money. Don't you?"

Desha laughed at his good-natured teasing. "More money might be a good thing for us all," she agreed.

Stephen engaged Desha in conversation for a few minutes before Elayne dragged her away. "Now, Stephen, don't monopolize her."

"Let me introduce her, Elayne," he said, grinning playfully. "You see to our other guests."

Elayne swatted him on the shoulder. "I don't trust you. We'll both introduce Desha."

Desha smiled and made all the right polite responses as she met the others. For the most part, she found them very pleasant. Several of the ladies expressed interest in her outfit and said they were coming by the shop next week. The men expressed interest in her clothes too, some teasingly asking if she could suggest something for their wives that would make them look like her.

Desha felt herself freeze when she, Elayne and Stephen stopped in front of Bryce and the blonde.

"You know Bryce, of course," Elayne said, "and this is Juliette Deuvux."

When Desha nodded, Bryce saw the bright glittering brown of her eyes. Of course, he reasoned, she was still upset about the way he had responded to her changes in *Southern Elegance*. His mother certainly could have told him beforehand that she had talked to Desha and given her permission. He had meant to apologize, but the truth was that he had been too cowardly. He had known all along that he couldn't see Desha again and walk away without becoming involved with her, very personally involved. *That* was the crux of the matter.

Desha spun around on her heel, surprised when a strolling band wandered out on the patio, followed by the caterers who began to place individual salads on the tables.

She couldn't keep the sparkle from her eyes. She had heard of such lavish affairs at rich people's homes, but she had never before seen one. The caterers were discreet as they poured wine in tall crystal glasses. The setting almost made her forget that Bryce was here with a woman. Almost.

"What can we get you to drink?" Stephen asked, his voice carrying well over the music. "We're having red wine with the meal."

"That will be fine," Desha said.

Stephen motioned to a circling waiter, lifted a glass off his tray, and handed it to Desha.

"Make yourself comfortable," Elayne invited, indicating a seat by Bryce. "You make her feel at home while I see about the food," she told her son.

"Here, sit down," Juliette insisted before Bryce could speak. "I want to hear all about your little showroom at *Southern Elegance*." She winked at Bryce. "Bryce has told me you made a real splash in the shop with your orange paint."

Bryce winced as his eyes met Desha's flashing brown ones. She told herself that she would like to help him make a real splash, right in the pool.

She smiled at Juliette, knowing she had no right to take her anger at Bryce out on the blonde. "It seems that Bryce has told you all about it," she said. "Has he also told you that I've already doubled business in a single week with my splashes of orange?"

Juliette widened green eyes. "No. He neglected to tell me that part."

"I see," Desha said, more disappointed than she wanted them to know. He had only told the part he thought sounded sensational.

"I must come into the store and see for myself," Juliette said. "You'll show me around, won't you, Bryce?"

"I'm sure Desha can do that," he said absently, his gaze holding the younger woman's. After he took Juliette home tonight, he would go by Desha's hotel and talk with her. They had to clear the air between them. He knew he didn't want Desha to stay angry with him.

"Dinner!" Elayne called out. "Everyone come and eat. Desha, sit with us, dear."

Breathing a sigh of relief, Desha made her way to Elayne's table. She told herself that she didn't care if she never saw Bryce Gerrard again as long as she lived! But it was a bald lie.

Stephen had barely seated her when a man sat down on her left. What rotten luck! It was Bryce, with Juliette, of course.

Deliberately giving her attention to the man on her right, Desha engaged him in lively conversation, and somehow she managed to get through the meal without speaking to Bryce.

After a delicious dessert and coffee had been served, someone tapped Desha on the shoulder. She turned around to see two men standing behind her. They both started to speak at the same time.

"Sorry, ol' boy," one told the other, "but I got here first."

He grinned winningly at Desha. "Please have pity on a bachelor and dance with me."

Desha looked hesitantly at Elayne. "Dance with the poor man, of course, if you'd like," she said. "Give this party some life." She winked at Desha. "It looks rather like *Southern Elegance* used to, doesn't it?"

Desha grinned, then briefly met Bryce's gaze. When she saw that he was glowering at her, she let the man pull back her chair and help her up. After they had crossed to the empty section of the tiled patio, she let him spin her around to the soft music of the strolling band. In minutes, several other couples were dancing.

But not Bryce. Seething with jealousy he hadn't known he was capable of, he stared at Desha while pretending to give his attention to Juliette. He felt like a rejected school boy, but he couldn't deny the green anger that swept through him as he watched Desha and Tom Lockwood dancing.

"You do remember my name, don't you?" Tom asked. "I remember yours—delicious Desha. It's time Elayne and Stephen invited some interesting people to their parties. Every time it's the same old crowd, so where did she find you, darling?"

Desha recalled that her horoscope had predicted romance today, but surely it hadn't meant this man. She didn't like the personal endearment, and she drew back a little in his arms.

"I remember your name, Mr. Lockwood," she said, "and Elayne found me at the shop."

He smiled. "Really? You're a salesclerk at Elayne's stuffy little shop?"

Desha was beginning to like this man less and less. She studied his face. Actually, he was quite attractive, blond, about thirty-five, and very well-dressed. It was his attitude she didn't care for.

"I happen to think very highly of the shop," she informed him, her voice tinged with annoyance. After all, she did think well of the shop, especially since she had altered it.

The man grinned at her. "Feisty little thing, aren't you? Well, don't get mad at me. I want to be your friend. I find you absolutely charming."

Desha didn't relax, but her anger did cool down a bit, despite his patronizing air. She glanced back over her shoulder at Bryce. Her eyes met his briefly before Tom spun her away again.

Desha sighed unhappily. She would much prefer to be in Bryce's arms. The moon was coming up. The air was cooling down. And this was the most romantic place she had ever been.

She was so lost in her thoughts that she didn't realize that Tom was leading her to the secluded end of the pool. One song led into another as he danced with her. At least he was a good dancer, she soothed herself, trying to forget about Bryce.

Suddenly Tom crushed her against his body, bent his head and tried to steal a kiss. She was so startled and so insulted that she immediately braced herself, grasped one of his arms and flipped him smoothly over her shoulder right into the swimming pool.

He landed with a big splash, fancy clothes and all. The band stopped playing and everyone looked around to see what had happened.

Desha didn't even wait to see if the man could swim. Furious and embarrassed, she marched across the tiles to the door leading into the house.

"Desha!" Elayne called. "Desha, what happened?"

When the woman didn't stop, Elayne chased after Bryce who was striding toward the pool. "Do find out what happened, Bryce," she urged.

"I know what happened," Bryce said through gritted teeth.

As Tom was struggling to climb the pool steps, Bryce lent him a helping hand. When the man was on his feet, Bryce clipped him across the jaw, sending him sprawling back into the water.

"Bryce!" Elayne cried. "What are you doing?"

"I'm gong to see about Desha," he said. "Tell Juliette I'll be right back."

Her mouth open in surprise, Elayne glanced back at the still struggling Tom, then gazed after Bryce in shock.

Bryce didn't see Desha anywhere. His jaw muscle working angrily, he climbed into his car. For a frustrating moment, he fumbled with his car keys, unable to find the one to the black Chrysler New Yorker he had purchased only yesterday. At last he found the right key and began to drive slowly down the street.

After a moment or two, he spotted Desha striding along, looking much too appealing in her colorful outfit.

"My heavens!" he groaned aloud. "Doesn't she have any sense? Wasn't Tom trouble enough?"

He slammed on his brakes and leaned over to open the passenger door. "Get in," he ordered.

"No thanks," she said in a clipped voice. "I've had enough of your charity to last me a lifetime. Leave me alone. I'll find my own way this time."

"Damn it, get in before I get out and drag you!" he ordered.

"Don't you try it or you'll find yourself in the same predicament as Mr. Lockwood," she threatened.

"Don't try your bravado on me," he snapped. "I'm in no mood for it. You'll find that I'm more man than you can handle. Now get in here!"

It suddenly occurred to Desha that Bryce Gerrard really might be more man than she could handle. "Oh, you—you—don't you threaten me. Just go back to your girlfriend! Leave me alone!" she cried.

Bryce shut off the engine and stepped out of the car. Before Desha could stride away, he grabbed her and drew her back to him. "You're coming with me. We need to talk."

"No! I'm not your type, remember? You like blondes. Go talk to Juliette!"

"My word, you try a man's patience!" Bryce snapped.

"And you try a woman's!" she flung at him. Her heart pounded, and she was near tears. She didn't understand Bryce's ability to make her respond so emotionally. "You owe me an apology! Several of them, and I won't talk to you until I hear them."

Bryce drew her closer. "Ah, Desha, you're impossible, you know that, don't you?" When he looked into her eyes, he saw the tears glistening there, and his anger began to cool. "But I suppose I do owe you an apology at that."

He freed her hands to caress her face. "I'm sorry about what happened there on the patio," he murmured. "I'm sorry about yelling at you at the shop. And I'm sorry I said you weren't my type. I'm afraid that was a lie."

When he saw her lips trembling, Bryce lowered his head and took possession of her mouth. He sighed as he drew her tightly to him, his hands sliding down over her hips.

Automatically locking her arms around his neck, Desha pressed her body closer to his as she met the fire in his kiss. After the single brief kiss he had given her before, this was what she had longed for. She would not be denied now, no matter what the circumstances or place.

When Bryce finally drew back from her, he said raggedly, "Please get in the car. We need to talk."

Nodding, Desha let him guide her inside. She wanted very much to hear what Bryce Gerrard had to say to her.

Chapter Six

"Why don't I take you by the hotel so you can change clothes," Bryce told Desha as he started the car. "I know a quiet spot where we can have a drink, relax and hear ourselves think."

He didn't want her to attract any other man's attention in that provocative outfit. It had created enough of a stir at the pool party. He didn't know what might happen if she wore it to a lounge, and he didn't want to find out. The next man he struck might not get off as easily as Tom.

Desha didn't know if she would ever be able to think again without remembering how Bryce's kiss felt against her lips, but she nodded her consent.

When he parked the car in the hotel parking lot, she asked, "Do you want to come up while I change?"

He smiled and shook his head. "No, I'll wait here." He didn't want her to know just how tempted he was to go up with her. He would like nothing better in the

world right now than to take her in his arms in the
privacy of her room. The thought was both heady and
dangerous.

"I'll only be a moment," she said, her eyes bright
with excitement.

As Bryce watched her walk away, moving easily on
the tall heels, her shapely legs eye-catching beneath the
bands of color in her skirt, he told himself that he had
heard that comment from women before, and it had
never been true. This time, however, he welcomed the
few minutes to himself. It would give him the breathing space he desperately needed.

Settling back against the seat, he closed his eyes and
wondered just what he was going to say to Desha. He
really didn't know, he only knew that he had to talk to
her. Seeing her tonight at the party had almost been
his undoing. It had bothered him that she was angry
with him, but it had bothered him even more seeing
her in Tom's arms.

He had realized that if any man kissed her, he
wanted it to be him, not Tom Lockwood. He could no
longer deny his attraction for her, but he wasn't sure
what he was going to do about it. If ever two people
were mismatched, he and Desha Smith were. That was
a fact, but logic didn't always take precedence over
emotion.

Up in her room, Desha searched frantically through
her few clothes, trying to find something appropriate. Anticipation of the night ahead flooded through
her while she discarded first one outfit, then another,
searching for she knew not what. She thought about
Bryce telling her that she was not his type, and she
wondered if Juliette Deuvux was. She hoped not. No,

she prayed not! As the piles of clothes mounted on the floor, she sighed in exasperation.

"Why am I driving myself crazy for that man?" she asked aloud. "Either I am his type, or I'm not, and if I'm not, all the clothes in the world won't change me."

She vowed to wear the next thing she touched, which just happened to be one of her more modest outfits.

"This might do," she murmured, wishing very much that she wasn't letting his taste influence what *she* wanted to wear. No matter how attracted she was to that man, she knew that she had to remain true to herself, if she were to be happy. And if she weren't happy, he wasn't going to be happy with her.

Despite her little pep talk, she also knew that she wanted very much to please him. She shivered as she recalled every tantalizing detail of his kiss. It made her dizzy to remember it, and surely a kiss that potent couldn't lie. If she wasn't his type, she didn't know who could be!

Eager to return to Bryce and determined to be as good as her word and only take a moment, Desha discarded her clothes in record time, pulling madly at the clinging bathing suit.

"Shucks," she complained impatiently. It was like fighting an octopus to get the snug suit off, and her hands were unsteady as it was. When she had succeeded in wrestling it down her legs, she let it fall to the floor with the other garments. She usually had more respect for clothing than this, but at the moment she couldn't afford the luxury.

Glancing at the big face of her watch, she saw that she had been gone four minutes. She made a quick dash to the bathroom to freshen her lipstick and run a comb through her hair, then hurried back through her room to the door. She glanced over her shoulder at the discarded clothes. The place was a royal mess. She was glad Bryce hadn't come up with her.

He barely had time to let his mind wander before, true to her word, Desha returned. He straightened in the car, his eyes on her as she walked across the parking lot. He had never known a woman to get dressed so quickly; but then he had never known a woman like Desha.

Now she wore a slim-skirted brown dress that showed off her figure to advantage, accenting her curving hips and small waist. The V neck revealed just a tantalizing glimpse of the golden beauty of her high, firm breasts. Bryce groaned as he vividly recalled the vision of Desha on the beach in her skimpy suit.

Did she know that she was driving him mad? Yes, she was attracted to him, too—he knew that from the first, and her kiss had more than confirmed it. But what now?

"You look lovely," he murmured, his gaze holding hers as she slid into the car beside him. The brown dress made her eyes look even darker, their color like rich brown velvet.

Desha smiled. Bryce had never given her a compliment, and she hadn't realized how much she had wanted one. "Thank you," she murmured. "I'm glad I found something that you like."

He smiled as he started the car. He liked a lot more about her than was wise to admit at the moment. He would just bide his time and see how the evening went.

The lounge Bryce had in mind was a small, isolated piano bar with a postage-stamp-sized dance floor. Done in white and gold, the room was intimate, with an understated elegance and a forties' charm. There were a few tables and several tall bar stools.

Bryce found a table at the back of the room. "Will this be all right?"

"Fine," Desha murmured.

When they had been served, Bryce settled back in his chair to gaze at Desha while she sipped a strawberry concoction. A small line of pink remained on her full upper lip when she set the glass down. He resisted the urge to wipe it away, watching instead as she daintily dabbed at the pink smudge with a paper napkin.

When the piano player began to play a sentimental love song, Desha uninhibitedly began to hum the words beneath her breath, swaying slightly to the music.

"I like that song," she told Bryce when she saw that he was looking at her intently.

"I gathered as much," he said, a playful smile on his mouth. "Would you like to dance to it?"

"Oh, Bryce, could we?" she asked eagerly. "I haven't danced in months until tonight, and I love to."

"Fine, shall we?"

He stood up and held out one hand. He needed to talk to her, but he realized that most of all, he wanted to hold her, to feel her lovely body against his, to just relax and enjoy her for a few moments. Too often when he was with her, he felt as though he were waging a war, either internally or externally, and tonight he didn't want that.

When Desha slipped her fingers into his, she felt those old familiar shivers up and down her spine. A rush of heat traveled through her, and she hoped Bryce couldn't feel the warmth in her hand. She felt breathless when he drew her into his arms on the tiny dance floor.

In her heels, she fit perfectly against his masculine contours, and she wasn't at all surprised to find that he was a polished and skillful dancer. Somehow she had expected no less of Bryce Gerrard.

When she looked into his eyes, she saw a bemused expression there. She tried to glance away but couldn't. She trembled as Bryce lowered his dark lashes to gaze down at her mouth. She became aware that she was breathing very rapidly and shallowly through parted lips. Trying to gain some control of her runaway senses, she inhaled slowly and deeply. The deep breath caused her breasts to press more firmly against Bryce's chest.

Involuntarily, Bryce responded to the soft pressure of Desha's body against his. Although he tried desperately to concentrate on the clear sweet notes of the instrumental as they floated around him, all he could think of was the woman in his arms. Holding her more tightly, he closed his eyes, drew her head to his shoulder, and let himself savor the moment.

A few other couples came onto the dance floor, but Bryce wasn't aware of anyone but the woman in his arms. As one song led to another, he and Desha moved in perfect harmony.

When the last song abruptly ended and the piano player announced that he was taking a short break, Bryce felt cheated. Reluctantly freeing Desha from his embrace, he kept one hand on her waist as he guided her back to their table.

"You dance beautifully, Desha," he said as he pulled out her chair.

She was delighted by the compliment. "Thank you. You do, too."

Bryce seated himself, then took a long swallow of his vodka and orange juice. "So, that's one thing we have in common," he said. "It's a start."

He set his drink down and leaned his elbows on the table, lacing his fingers together in front of him. "Desha, I don't think two people could be less suited to each other than we are, but I don't seem to have any other choice but to see what happens with us."

He groaned inwardly as the dreamy expression in her eyes faded, and he wondered how on earth he had managed to state his position so ineptly. He had intended to tell her that he simply couldn't resist her, but somehow the words didn't come out right.

Really romantic, Gerrard, he told himself sarcastically while he tried to think of some plausible way to rephrase the statement.

Desha stared out the window, pretending to be interested in something on the street so that he wouldn't see her unhappiness. She had thought they were doing just fine together. Sure, their sun signs said they were opposites, but everything inside her said that this man could be the one for her. She wasn't foolish enough to tell Bryce that. Clearly she was letting her emotions rule her head.

"I'm sorry you feel that way," she murmured, glancing at him. She stood up abruptly. "I'd like to leave now, Bryce."

"Oh, Lord," he said aloud, wondering why he hadn't been more tactful. He wasn't usually a man who fumbled his words and thoughts. Maybe it did have something to do with the stars. His surely seemed to be giving him trouble.

He reached for her hand, but she crossed her arms, afraid to have him touch her again. She was trembling, and she didn't want him to know how much he had upset her, how much this night had meant to her.

"Sit down, Desha. Stay awhile longer."

She turned her gaze back to the window, sure that the tears ready to spring to her eyes would betray her. She couldn't stay. She couldn't let Bryce know how vulnerable she was. It wasn't at all like her to take such a tumble for a man who didn't truly care for her. She had her pride.

Suddenly, she saw a blue truck passing by on the street. The robber! He was just the excuse she needed to get out of this awkward predicament, these emotionally explosive circumstances. He would buy her a little time to get herself together again. And maybe she couldn't do anything about her situation with Bryce, but perhaps she could do something about the robbery.

"Hurry!" she cried to Bryce. "Let's get the car!"

Bryce studied her animated features. He seemed to have missed a beat here. He had been sure that Desha was upset because of what he had said. But maybe he was wrong.

"Why? What's the hurry?"

Desha pointed to the street. "That's the robber in that blue truck. He's getting away. Let's follow him!"

Unable to believe he was doing it, yet caught up in the urgency of her request, Bryce did as she asked. Together they rushed to the car and raced off into the night, although it was against Bryce's deepest instincts. At least, he told himself, he could get the license number to give to the police.

With Desha leaning forward tensely, straining to keep the truck in sight in the night traffic, Bryce headed down the busy Virginia Beach street in pursuit. Weaving their way in and out of traffic, they finally caught up with the vehicle as it turned off onto a less congested street.

Bryce couldn't see the driver's face, but he could see that there were two people in the truck. "Are you sure that's the one?" he asked, as they closed the gap. He tried his best to make out the license number, but the plate was mud-splattered.

As the vehicles traveled down the street, the truck driver glanced over his shoulder. Suddenly, he stepped on the gas, speeding away, leaving Bryce far behind. Curiosity piqued, believing that Desha did indeed have the right truck now, Bryce speeded up. Abruptly, the truck veered off onto an even less traveled road, kicking up clouds of dust as it raced along, sometimes riding on the shoulder.

"Oh, hurry, Bryce! Hurry! He's getting away!" Desha cried, urging him on.

"We don't want an accident, even to find out who your robber is, Desha," he told her, but now he was determined to discover if this was indeed the robber. After all, the man was in a big hurry for some reason.

Pressing his foot more firmly to the pedal, Bryce caught up with the wavering vehicle at the end of the winding road. The driver finally pulled over to the side and stopped.

"You wait here," Bryce told Desha as he slid out of the car.

"I want to see if that's him," she insisted. "He's not getting away from me this time!"

Before Bryce could reach her, she climbed out of the car and marched toward the truck.

Exasperated, Bryce swiftly caught up with her and spun her around. "I asked you to wait in the car."

"But, Bryce, you don't know what the man looks like!"

"*Please*," he said tightly, "will you just wait in the car." He didn't know what he would find in that truck and he didn't want her there. If *he* had any sense, he would go back and call the police, but he reasoned that Desha had to get this robber out of her system so that she could get on with her life.

And he had a feeling that he would be better off when this was over, too. He had to find some way to have a meeting of the minds with Desha.

Desha grudgingly did as he asked. She didn't like anyone making her decisions for her, but after all, she told herself, he had followed the truck as she had asked. She could do this one thing he wanted, even if she didn't agree with it.

When Bryce reached the other vehicle, he saw that the windows were rolled up and the couple inside was huddled together, talking to each other. He wondered if he had lost his mind to be here doing this.

"Hello in there," he called out, rapping sharply on the window.

The man jumped and whirled around in the seat to stare at him. To Bryce's amazement, he recognized the face of his elderly neighbor at the same time as the man recognized him.

"Oh, Bryce," the other man murmured, rolling down his window in obvious relief. "Am I glad to see that it's you!"

"Calvin!" Bryce said. "What are you doing here?"

"What am I doing here?" he asked, peering at Bryce through his glasses. "Why, trying to get away from you. We didn't know it was you, and I don't mind telling you that you scared us half to death. Lizzie and I didn't know what to do when you kept chasing us." He laughed nervously. "I didn't recognize your car. Must be another new one, huh?"

Deeply embarrassed, Bryce nodded. "Yes, I just bought it. I didn't recognize this truck either."

"We don't often drive it, but our car's in the shop," Calvin explained, then asked in a nervous voice, "Has something happened, Bryce? Is there something wrong at the house? Why were you following us like that?"

If Bryce could have sunk into the road and disappeared, he would have. How did he explain to this elderly man and his wife that he had chased them because Desha thought Calvin was a robber?

He sighed wearily and wished his conscience didn't prohibit lying. "I'm sorry, Calvin, Lizzie," he said, nodding to the woman. "It was all a mistake." He didn't know when he had felt like a bigger fool.

"I'm with a lady friend," he said tightly, looking back at the car, fully expecting Desha to bound from it at any minute and try to give poor old Mr. Crawford a lesson in jujitsu. "She thought she recognized the truck."

He didn't have the heart to go into the tale of the robber, and he was more than thankful that Desha remained in the car. He could just imagine her repeating the story, enlivening it a little more this time for the old couple.

"Gee, Bryce, if we had known it was you, I wouldn't have driven so fast," Calvin explained. "Lizzie was frightened just about out of her wits." He grinned a little and patted the woman's knee. "Too much television, huh, Lizzie?"

She smiled shyly at Bryce. "Come visit us when you have time, Bryce. We don't see much of you, but then I know you're busy."

He ran a hand through his short hair and thought about how he felt like shaking Desha at the moment. He had pursued the truck in part because he knew she was upset with him over his thoughtless statement, and he had wanted to do something to smooth her ruffled feathers. "Thank you, Lizzie. I'll have to make some time to visit."

He really was too busy for socializing with his aged neighbors who had turned their farm over to hired help and had nothing but time on their hands. While he liked them and truly enjoyed chatting with them, he'd been too busy lately to visit with them.

"Now you do that, Bryce," Calvin said. "And say hello to your mother for us."

Bryce nodded and waited for the truck to drive off. He wasn't at all surprised to see Desha jump out of the car and run toward him.

"What happened? Why is he leaving? Did he confess?" Desha asked excitedly, the words tumbling from her lips.

Bryce drew in a steadying breath and tightened his fingers around hers as he led her back to the car. "That wasn't your robber. It—"

"It *was* my robber!" she insisted. "And you let him get away. Shucks, Bryce, I told you I should go to the truck."

"And I told you I didn't want you to," he retorted, fast losing patience. "Desha, that was my elderly neighbor, Calvin Crawford and his wife, Lizzie. We almost scared them silly chasing after them like that. It was a foolish thing to do, and I can't tell you how embarrassed I am that I was a party to it."

The information calmed Desha down momentarily. She didn't say anything while Bryce opened the front door for her and she got back into the car, but she was thinking plenty.

Bryce's lips were set in a tight line when he slid back in on the driver's side. His features were briefly outlined in the light of the car as he opened and closed the door. "I think I should take you home. I believe we've had enough futile adventure for one night."

"Futile adventure! That's hardly what I call it. That was the truck the robber was driving the day I was robbed. I would recognize it anywhere."

Bryce tried his best to keep his temper in check, but there was something recklessly passionate about this woman that caused him to act in kind. "I think you were mistaken. That was not the truck. After all," he added more quietly, "you were upset that day, and you didn't see a license number."

She was upset now, more upset than she wanted to admit, and she knew that it was a culmination of the evening's events. She had been upset since Bryce told her how he felt about her in the lounge. She wanted him to believe her about the truck. It was important to her.

"I tell you that was the truck."

"And I tell you it wasn't!" he declared with finality. "Desha, you know you're prone to act rashly."

"Rashly?" she repeated, wishing she could see his face better in the scant light. "Exactly what do you mean by that?" It seemed that she couldn't do anything to please him, and she did want to, badly. "Are you referring to me painting the store?"

He sighed, not sure himself what he was referring to. This wasn't at all the evening he had anticipated when he took her to the hotel to change clothes, but they might as well clear the air here and now. He did know he was referring to a lot more than her painting the shop.

"I mean rashly," he declared. "I mean unreasonably. I mean chasing robbers; I mean living in a hotel you can't afford; I mean gypsying all over the country. You live your life without thought or order, colorfully, just like you dress, traveling about the country according to whichever whim catches your fancy."

Desha straightened her back proudly and turned fully in her seat to face him. "And who are you to judge me?" she cried. "You—you stuffy, staid, stinker of a man!" She couldn't recall when she had last been so hurt or insulted. "Look at you! Living on the fringes of life with no spontaneity at all, afraid to step out of your orderly, monied, bandbox existence, accusing me of dressing *colorfully*!"

She took a deep breath and continued. "Well, I'll tell you something, Bryce Gerrard! If you want me to be like everybody else—like you—traveling the same narrow path of life, dressed in look-alike clothes, afraid to step out of line, afraid to take a chance and live for fear of looking the fool, you can think again! I can't think of anything more dull than a world, and attitude, like that!"

"I'm not asking you to be like everybody else," he said, trying to temper both his and her anger. Now he was as insulted as she. *Stuffy, staid, stinker* of a man, indeed! Had this slip of a female, with no direction in her life really said that to him? "I'll have you know that I've taken plenty of chances in my time. How do you think I got where I am today in the business world?"

"I really don't even know where you are!" she flung at him. And furthermore, at the moment, she didn't want to know.

"Well, let me enlighten you. I worked diligently, from the time I graduated from college—after working my way through, by the way—and parlayed a small bankroll into a million-dollar business."

She frowned, her anger subsiding only the slightest bit. She remembered thinking that Bryce managed his mother's money. She had assumed that the family fortune had come from his mother's shops, but obviously it was the other way around. She did recall Elayne saying that Bryce bought the shop for her. And she did admire him for accomplishing what she herself hoped to achieve. But it didn't make all that much difference at the moment.

"Well, I hope you and your success will be very happy together because you seem to be married to it." She didn't know why she had used that particular phrase, but she rushed on. "We're back to square one, aren't we? Bryce and Desha: the bull and the ram— definitely incompatible."

"I did not call you a ram," he retorted, "and I don't appreciate being called a bull. I don't think we have to resort to name-calling."

Desha didn't know whether she should laugh or cry, but she could feel tears building at the back of her eyes. She had been on the verge of weeping all evening, and it was getting harder and harder to hold back the flood. How stupidly she had reacted to this man's kiss, building plans and hopes on a moment of desire! And now she was about to disgrace herself by crying!

"I was referring to our sun sign symbols," she said thickly. "Now I really do want you to take me home."

As he watched her draw herself up proudly, he realized that once again he had gone about this all wrong. So they were the bull and the ram. Well, he still didn't think they were totally incompatible.

Sure, they were mismatched in a lot of areas, substantial areas, but they were matched in others, and he didn't mean only physically. When he looked at her, hurt and vulnerable, yet still with that shield of invincibility all around her, he wanted to take her home. To his home, and make everything right between them.

"Desha," he said without thinking, "why don't you come home with me? I have a little cottage on my land, a safe distance from the house, I assure you, where you can stay until you're more financially secure."

At first she thought she hadn't heard him correctly, but no, he had said what she had thought he had. She had heard him quite well.

"You can't be serious!" she cried, her brown eyes glittering. "I've taken my last bit of charity from you, and I hope that's not what this night is all about. I will not live in your cottage, no matter how far from the house it is. I've had enough of your charity and your protectiveness. All I want is for you to take me home, and if you're not willing to do that, I'll get out and walk."

Bryce had no doubt in the world that she would, but he was going to have his say first. Then, by heaven above, he *would* take this unreasonable woman back to her hotel. He hadn't been offering her charity, he had just been using common sense and trying to do the practical thing. He was worried about her, and he did feel protective toward her. But he couldn't seem to do *anything* to please her!

He thought that she had surely confused their sun sign symbols. She was the bull—stubborn, impossible—and he was the ram—butting his head against the wall.

"You know, Desha, for once I wish you'd just listen to me and see that I'm only trying to do what's best for you. All of this came about because you insisted I chase that blue truck," he said. "It's a prime example of the way you live your life. Sure, the robbery was an injustice, but sometimes in life, we have to put those kinds of injustices behind us and go on. You can't defend yourself against the whole world just because you claim to know jujitsu, and you can't correct every injustice in life."

"Do you really feel that way?" she demanded, balling her hands into fists. "Well, that sounds just like you, Bryce. Thank heavens everyone doesn't take that stance! I can't believe that you're advocating letting criminals run the streets just because everyone wants to look the other way. That robber is not going to go unpunished, if I have to hunt for him day and night. And that *was* his truck we chased!"

Bryce groaned audibly. The wall again. He had simply tried to point out an indisputable fact of life about injustice, and now she had him advocating letting criminals run free.

The key grated in the ignition when he started the car. In minutes they had left the isolated road and were headed toward the busy streets of the city. Stung by

Desha's outbursts, Bryce told himself that he couldn't get her back to the hotel fast enough to suit him.

When he had driven up in front of the hotel, he leaned across Desha to open her door at the same time as she reached for the handle. Bryce's fingers closed over hers, and he felt the warmth of her trembling hand.

Desha quickly snatched her fingers back, but not soon enough to stop the shivers that ran up and down her arm at Bryce's touch. How could she still react so intensely to him? she asked herself.

When he had opened the door, she studiously avoided his gaze as she hurried out of the car, her dress hem rising in her haste. Slamming the door behind her, she marched away without looking back a single time.

She couldn't. Her vision was blurred by her tears and she couldn't seem to catch her breath. She didn't want to see Bryce again. So why did she feel like she was leaving the most important part of her life behind in his car?

As Bryce gazed after her, his heart beat intensely. It was all for the best that she had refused his offer to stay at the cottage. It was all for the best that they had quarreled and gotten it over with. It had been inevitable. She didn't like his life-style, and he didn't like hers.

So why did he feel like she was stepping all over his heart when he watched her walk away? Why did he feel like he should run after her and beg her to listen just once more, until he could make her understand how he felt and why he had said those things to her?

Throwing the car into gear, he stomped on the gas and sped away from the hotel, not having the slightest idea where he was going. He was five miles down the street before he remembered that he'd left Juliette at his mother's pool party. Glancing down at his watch, he saw that that had been over two hours ago. He groaned again. He might as well get this over with, too.

Chapter Seven

Once the tears which had been threatening all evening began to fall, Desha was helpless to hold back the tide. As they cascaded down her cheeks in a torrent like she'd never known, she ran upstairs to her room. She couldn't help remembering that Bryce had said she couldn't afford the hotel, and she was even more distressed. Who did he think he was, trying to run her life? Trying to tell her what she could and couldn't afford, what she should and shouldn't do?

She had left home years ago, and she didn't need someone laying out her life for her. She didn't know how she had kept quiet long enough to listen. But worse than that, why was she fool enough to care what he had said?

What she really needed, she conceded, was someone to *share* her life. Suddenly, she was weary of making her way alone, of dreaming her dreams by herself. The thought was as startling and disturbing as the rest of the evening had been. Why on earth did she have to decide such a thing now at the end of this especially disastrous night?

She caught sight of her reflection in the mirror. When she saw the image of the weeping woman in the brown dress and heels she had thought would please Bryce, she ripped the garment off and flung it down among the rest of the clothes she had hurriedly discarded when she dressed for him. Had it only been a couple of hours ago? It seemed like a lifetime. She had rushed out of this room with such eager expectation, and what had she gotten?

Brushing angrily at the tears that still tumbled down her face unchecked, she began to hiccup as she rummaged around in the clothes until she uncovered her bathrobe. Colorful, he had called her! She looked at the red, orange and green striped robe as she slid it on over her panties and bra. And what was wrong with color?

She had meant it when she told Bryce that she didn't want to be like everyone else in the world—like him with his narrow views and restricted styles. She had meant it when she told him that he lived on the fringes of life, and that it wasn't for her. She'd meant every word of it.

So why was she so miserably and desperately unhappy now that she had put him in his place and sent him on his way? Why did she feel so empty and alone? The bull and the ram again, butting head to head, totally opposite, an impossible match. So why didn't her heart understand?

She glanced at the mirror again. The brown dress was gone. The colorful Desha was back. And this one was sobbing just as hard as the other one. After kicking off her heels, she curled up on her bed in the rented room and let the tears come.

Bryce was shocked to realize that he had completely forgotten all about Juliette as the events of the night unfolded. If his mother's message that Juliette wasn't the woman for him hadn't penetrated, at least his message to himself should. If Juliette could be so easily forgotten in the space of the two hours he had been with Desha, wasn't it time they both recognized that the romance wasn't viable and went their separate ways?

He ran his hands through his hair as he pulled up into his mother's driveway. Funny, no matter what Elayne had said, he thought the romance with Juliette had been taking a natural enough course. And hadn't it been natural enough for him, for his—what was it Desha had called his life-style?—for his staid, stuffy life, for his monied, bandbox existence?

Damn that woman! Her insults still rankled. In fact, they rankled as no other he could ever remember. He lived his own life, the way he saw fit; he had never really given one whit what someone else thought about it, had he? So why was he so upset over what some flighty female like Desha Smith said about him? He didn't believe it, of course, but it irked him all the same that she had managed to insult him so thoroughly in the space of five minutes.

"That's gratitude for you," he grumbled to himself as he opened his car door and climbed out. "That'll teach you to try to do a kind deed, to try to help some stray stranger."

But as he walked to the door, he realized that the last thing he thought of Desha was as a stray stranger...the very last thing.

"Bryce, honey, where have you been?" Elayne cried, spying him as he entered the house. She crossed the length of the hall with long graceful strides. "Where's Desha?" she asked, glancing behind him. "Is she all right? Did you find her?"

Gritting his teeth, Bryce tried to think of something sane, something civil to say to his mother about the woman he had gone after with such good intentions. The music and the animated chatter of the party still in full bloom out on the patio drifted toward him.

"She's back at her hotel."

"I don't understand what happened," Elayne said, her blue eyes troubled. "What did poor Tom do?"

"He tried to kiss her."

Elayne breathed a sigh of relief. "My word, I thought he'd done something truly abominable."

"That was abominable enough," Bryce said, his anger surging anew at the thought. "He's lucky I didn't break his neck."

"Oh?" Elayne murmured, her eyes suddenly bright as she studied her son's angry face. "Harsh punishment for a man trying to steal a kiss from a woman you don't care much for, isn't it?"

Bryce's jaw muscle twitched. "His behavior was in extremely bad taste, and was totally unwanted and unwarranted."

Elayne smiled slightly. "Desha's a very pretty girl. I suppose the poor man was just so smitten that he couldn't help himself. It's a good thing you were there to protect her."

The blue eyes so like his mother's were stormy. "She didn't need my protection," he snapped. "She's more than capable of taking care of herself, or so *she* assures me."

Elayne chuckled. "You two quarreled."

"It's not funny," he said tightly. "She's impossible. I don't know why I bother with her. She's been a thorn in my side since the day I had the misfortune to meet her at that damned toll booth."

"Thank God, I think I know why," Elayne breathed with an exaggerated sigh of relief. "It sounds like something vaguely familiar, sort of like love."

"Don't be ridiculous!" he declared. "I'm not in love with the woman."

"I don't want to be the one to tell you, son," his mother said sweetly, "but that thorn you think you feel is probably more like an arrow. Cupid's arrow. I think I mentioned Cupid to you recently. You can't escape him."

"Ha!" Bryce said without merriment. "I've never known the little creature, nor do I want to. You're the one determined to see me in love with someone."

"Not just someone," his mother corrected. "The right someone, and I'm not the one who's overseeing this romance between you and Desha. I'm just an interested bystander."

"Mother," he said crisply, "there is *no* romance!" Embarrassed, he looked over his shoulder to make sure that no one was within hearing distance. "We don't even *like* each other."

Elayne wasn't swayed in her assessment of the situation. "You don't have to like each other to be in love, but let me tell you it sure makes things run more smoothly."

"Are you listening to anything I've said?" he demanded. "The woman is difficult at best—impossible at worst. We couldn't get along in a million years. She's reckless and irresponsible. She's rash, and she's also rude."

Elayne arched an exquisite brow. "My goodness, that sounds like a rehearsed speech. Have you given it recently? And what nice things does she have to say about you?" she asked, tongue in cheek.

Bryce briefly closed his eyes and sighed raggedly. The words were still crystal clear in his mind. "That I live on the fringes of life with no spontaneity at all, afraid to leave my monied, bandbox existence. That I travel a narrow path, afraid to step out of line, afraid to take a chance and live for fear of looking the fool. That I'm a *staid, stuffy, stinker* of a man!"

Elayne tried to stifle a giggle, but it got the best of her. "My, my, but she did say a mouthful. What on earth brought about this little exchange? You were jealous over Tom, weren't you?"

"It wasn't that," he denied, then immediately realized that he was lying not only to her, but to himself as well. "You won't believe this," he said, wondering if he had lost his sanity even to tell her, "but I let Desha talk me into chasing what she thought was the robber down the streets of Virginia Beach."

"On foot?" she asked.

"No, not on foot. By car."

"How exciting!" Elayne said, eyes bright.

"Damn it, Mother, it wasn't exciting. It was foolish, and could have been dangerous as well. As it turned out, of all the people in this town, it was Calvin and Lizzie I chased."

"Crawford?" she asked.

Shaking his head at the memory, he nodded. "Can you believe it?"

"Well, you know the old saying: it is a small world," she murmured. "I wonder why on earth Desha thought it was the Crawfords who robbed her?"

"She didn't think it was them," Bryce explained tiredly, wondering why he had begun this story. "She insisted they were driving the truck the robber drove. Do you see now how absurd the whole thing is, how irresponsible the woman is?"

He shook his head. "And she accused me of advocating letting criminals run the streets because I told her how futile it was to chase after a truck she *thought* the robber had driven. Can you believe she said that, among the other little compliments she paid me?" he said dryly.

Pursing her lips, Elayne was pensive for a moment. Then, to Bryce's utter irritation, she nodded. "Yes, I can believe it. And not only that, I agree."

"You *what*?" he exclaimed.

"I agree with Desha," she said calmly, totally disregarding his outraged expression. "You know, Bryce, it's not enough that you've achieved so much success so young. You *have* become stuffy and rigid. I've told you that myself, in so many words."

"Well, I'll be damned, if you aren't as bad as she is," he said, incredulous.

When she saw the annoyed look on his face, she hastily added, "Now please don't get me wrong. You're a fine, decent human being and no son could have been more wonderful to any mother, but you've fallen into these set patterns now that you've become successful. And what good is success and what it brings if you don't have someone to share it with?

Why, I think Desha's the most wonderful thing that's happened to you. You can deny it all you want, but you're in love with that girl."

"Love!" Bryce scoffed. "I think you'd pair me up with Cinderella's stepsisters if you thought they could give you grandchildren."

"Not true," she said. "I only want you to marry *one* woman. Cinderella had *two* stepsisters." When Bryce wasn't amused, she added, "Seriously, I only want your happiness. Juliette isn't for you. She never was."

"Oh, my God," he said, exhaling wearily. "I forgot about Juliette again!"

"Again?" Elayne murmured.

"Where is she?" Bryce asked, turning toward the patio.

"She's not here," his mother said, catching him by the arm. "She gave Tom a ride home." She arched her brows slightly. "She was rather angry with you for running off like that, Bryce."

He shook his head. "I'm angry with myself. The whole evening was handled badly, but you're right," he admitted. "Juliette isn't for me. I think we're overdue for a long talk."

Elayne couldn't conceal her pleased smile. "I think it's all for the best."

He nodded. "You would say that. Good night, Mother."

"Good night, Son."

Bryce gave her a quick kiss on the cheek, then vanished out the door. He wasn't ready to face the evening ahead, but it was inevitable.

* * *

Lying in his bed hours later, Bryce reviewed the
devastating evening. Juliette had been anything but
calm about his suggestion that they go their separate
ways. Contrary to his mother's observations, Juliette's blood could boil when she thought she'd been
wronged, and although she had been perfectly content with the status quo, she didn't like in the least the
prospect of losing Bryce altogether.

She had reached the same erroneous conclusion that
Elayne had; she believed that there was something
promising going on between him and Desha, and she
hadn't liked being in second place one bit.

Bryce had felt badly about the entire situation, but
regardless of what precipitated it, he did believe that
it was time he and Juliette faced the fact that there was
no future for them. He had, however, hotly denied
that he was in love with Desha.

It wasn't until he found himself restlessly tossing
and turning in his bed at three a.m. that he finally admitted the sad truth: he *was* falling in love with Desha. Of course it would never work, and it was all for
the best that they had realized that tonight. Still, the
realization did nothing to soothe the unfamiliar ache
in his heart.

All the reasoning in the world didn't change the way
Desha had stirred his soul when he kissed her, or the
way she had molded so tantalizingly and perfectly to
his body. In truth, she had been right when she told
him that he wanted her to be more like his ideal
woman so that she could fit neatly into his life. The
mere thought was so ridiculous as to be laughable.
Desha was definitely Desha, and he was Bryce, whatever opposing mold that put them into.

But he wasn't laughing. For the first time in years, he felt like crying. Miserable, he closed his eyes and fought for healing sleep.

Desha could hardly get up the next morning. She felt as if she hadn't slept a single wink, and the last place in the world she wanted to go was to Bryce's mother's shop. Not that she didn't enjoy the shop, she told herself; in fact, she took great pride in her modest role in increasing business, but the shop tied her to Bryce, and she didn't want that.

Her phone had rung off the hook until almost midnight, but she hadn't answered it, sure that it was Bryce. Now she was more sorry that she hadn't taken the cheapest hotel room she could find. If she had even an extra hundred dollars, she would get Betty repaired and strike out for God only knew where.

She sighed, knowing she wasn't being honest, not even with herself. The truth was that she didn't really want to travel on. It was the craziest thing, but she wanted to stay right here, and even though she tried to tell herself that it was just the place that she liked, there was no denying that Bryce played a role in her desire to stay.

Could it be possible that she, Desha Smith, one-time hopeful actress, current hopeful business whiz, had gone and given her heart and her dreams to a man? And Bryce Gerrard of all men? Had she fallen in love with him? The notion was too painful to pursue.

As she did every morning, she picked up the paper outside her door to read her horoscope. She noted with mild interest that she was to encounter new business possibilities today. Suddenly she threw the paper down in disgust; hadn't she expected romance last night because of what her horoscope had said? And what had she gotten?

Still, she was in a somewhat improved mood by the time she reached the shop, even if she wasn't her usual enthusiastic self. Maybe, just maybe, there was a new business venture on the horizon and she could leave *Southern Elegance & not so elegants*, but still stay in town. She would not admit, even to herself, that she still harbored the hope that she and Bryce could somehow work through their differences.

The phone was ringing when she unlocked the door, and she muttered a few curses about customers who couldn't even wait until store hours to start phoning.

"Hello. *Southern Elegance & not so elegants*," she said when she picked up the receiver.

"Desha." Elayne's voice radiated warmth and concern. "How are you? I was so worried about you last night. Bryce said you had returned to your hotel, but I couldn't reach you by phone. I don't know how to begin to apologize for the behavior of my guest at the party. It wasn't at all like Tom."

So, Bryce hadn't been the one trying to reach her last night. Desha experienced a definite sinking feeling inside, and it was all she could do to concentrate on the conversation at hand.

"It wasn't your fault, Elayne," she said, sighing heavily. "Please don't feel responsible. I—I shouldn't have even been there."

In the aftermath of the poolside incident, she had to admit that she wasn't guiltless. After all, if she hadn't been hoping to make Bryce jealous, maybe Tom wouldn't have felt that he could kiss her and get away with it.

"You had every right to be there," Elayne said soothingly. "Tom was totally in the wrong, and I intend to see that he apologizes."

"Please don't do that," Desha urged. "It's really not necessary."

Elayne chuckled. "Well, I think he learned his lesson anyway. When Juliette drove him home, he was dripping wet."

"Juliette?" Desha murmured, unable to help herself.

"Yes, you met her." There was a deliberate pause. "Bryce's ex-girlfriend."

Desha had to bite her tongue to keep from repeating that statement.

"Desha, could you find time to have lunch with me today?" Elayne continued as though she hadn't dropped such a tantalizing tidbit of information. "I'd really like to talk to you."

"I'm sorry," Desha said quickly, "but I don't think so. I don't think we have anything to talk about," she said honestly, believing that Elayne wanted to talk about Bryce. Desha just couldn't stand it today.

"But we do," Elayne insisted calmly. "I want to discuss the store. It's very important. We need to talk, if not over lunch, there at the shop. I much prefer lunch. Do say you'll join me."

Desha's fingers tightened around the phone. The store? What had her horoscope said? New business opportunities? Yet, as much as she believed that her destiny was controlled by the stars, she brushed aside any thought of Elayne proposing a new business opportunity.

Bryce's mother had probably decided to let her go. How could she refuse the lunch invitation? Bryce had no doubt had a hand in this, but perhaps it was all for the best.

"All right. I usually eat at the fast-food restaurant on the corner. How about there?"

"I'd thought perhaps we could try something just a little more substantial," Elayne said tactfully. "I'd like to take you to a small place I know of, if that's all right. Norman could pick you up at one."

Desha found herself agreeing against her better judgment. "I'll be ready."

"That's wonderful, Desha," the other woman said. "I'll see you then."

When Desha replaced the phone, she couldn't contain a totally inexplicable twinge of anticipation. Shaking her head, she set about her work again, unable to squelch that small voice that told her she was eager to hear what Elayne had to say.

The hours didn't pass quickly enough to suit her. A little before one, she put the Out to Lunch sign on the door and went to the small employee's rest room to freshen her makeup. As she gazed at her reflection, she wished she had worn something different to work.

With a shrug, she turned away. She could no more please Elayne Hammond with her dress than she could Bryce. Hadn't she learned her lesson last night?

Norman rapped on the outside door promptly at the appointed hour. The chauffeur wore such a big smile that Desha couldn't help but smile in return as she closed the shop door behind her.

"How are you today, Norman?" she asked brightly.

"Real good. And you, Miss Smith?"

"I'm all right."

"Well, I'll make sure to behave myself," he said with a twinkle in his eye. "I heard from the staff about

you tossing Mr. Lockwood into the pool last night.''
He gestured to his immaculate uniform. ''These are
provided, but I'd hate to get this one wet.''

Desha smiled. ''Wasn't that awful of me? Is there
anyone in Virginia Beach who doesn't know about
that?''

''Not if the house staff can help it,'' he said, grinning at her. ''We haven't had such good gossip in
years.''

Desha opened her door and climbed in before Norman could assist her. He waited until she had pulled
it shut, then made sure it was properly closed.

When he parked in front of a small but exclusive
restaurant a few minutes later, Desha drew in her
breath. ''Oh, Norman, is this where I'm to meet Mrs.
Hammond? It looks so stuffy.''

''I'm told it's a very fine restaurant, Miss Smith.
I'm sure Mrs. Hammond anticipates a pleasant meal.''

Desha put a smile on her face. ''Of course she does.
I'm just not dressed for this.'' She made a wry face.
''But then I don't suppose I would be, no matter what
I wore.''

She reached for the door handle, but Norman spoke
before she could open the door. ''Please let me open
the door for you.''

''Yes, of course,'' she replied, a taint of pink on her
cheeks. He was the chauffeur; he wanted to do his job,
to handle his responsibilities, just as she wanted to
handle hers.

''Thank you,'' she said politely as he smiled at her.

''You're welcome. Enjoy your lunch, Miss Smith.''

Elayne was sitting at a window table near the front.
She waved to Desha when the younger woman entered the room.

Glancing around, Desha was even more impressed by the inside of the restaurant than the outside. The height of luxury, it was beautifully decorated, from the pale salmon walls to the peach tablecloths.

"This is quite lovely," Desha said, joining Elayne, "but I'm sure it's dreadfully expensive."

"It is," Elayne said unabashedly.

Desha gazed into the other woman's blue eyes and was immediately reminded of Bryce. She glanced down at the open menu before her.

"We really should have gone to a fast-food restaurant," she murmured.

"Why?" Elayne asked, a warm smile on her face. 'I have plenty of money, and I worked darned hard with the shops to get it. Why shouldn't I spend some of it? I've put away more for rainy days than I'll ever use. I certainly don't need to leave it to Bryce. He's got more than I have now. So why not spend it?"

Desha was taken aback by the woman's revelations, but before she could think of anything to say, Elayne looked around the lovely restaurant, then smiled at the approaching waiter. "This is one of my favorite spots in the city. I love these surroundings."

"I can understand why," Desha agreed.

"What would you like to eat?" Elayne asked, as the waiter came to the table and stood patiently while Desha scanned the menu.

When Desha had ordered and the man had gone, Elayne leaned forward and laughed softly. "I've had such a wonderful time watching my shops grow and prosper, especially *Southern Elegance*," she said, her eyes holding Desha's. "It wasn't always easy, but I can't think of any work I could have loved more. I take great pride in what I accomplished, and I truly believe it was only possible because I cared so much."

"I'm sure that's true," Desha agreed. "And you have a right to be proud. *Southern Elegance* is a fine shop."

Elayne winked. "So you say now, but you didn't think that when you first went to work there."

A shy smile on her lips, Desha nodded, "No, but I do love it now. All it needed was a dash of color and a little change in stock," she said. "The rest was already there."

"You really do enjoy the shop, don't you?" Elayne asked, her tone more serious, her eyes carefully watching Desha.

Desha nodded. "I can't think of any other work I'd rather do either. I tried acting, but it wasn't quite me. I need to have a product instead of be one. You know I had my own shop in South Carolina. Losing it was a big disappointment, but I'll succeed in the financial world yet. My horoscope assures it."

"You do believe that, don't you?" Elayne asked.

"It's my destiny," Desha said, brown eyes wide and solemn. "We can't change fate, Mrs. Hammond."

"Please, it's Elayne. I have a feeling we're going to be very good friends, Desha. Surely we can use our first names."

"I'd like that very much," Desha said. "You know, Elayne, I haven't had a chance to thank you for standing up for me at the shop when Bryce was so..."

Her words trailed off. After all, this was the man's mother.

Elayne couldn't hide the pleasure she found in this frank young woman. "He was a stinker that day, wasn't he?"

Lowering long, dark lashes, Desha wondered if the use of the term "stinker" was coincidental, or if Bryce had told his mother about their conversation last night.

"Yes," Elayne said, not keeping her guessing, "Bryce told me you two quarreled last night."

Both women looked up when their food was served. Elayne picked up her fork and began to casually eat as she discussed her son's behavior. "Of course I've known him much longer than you have, and I can vouch for what a fine man he is, but we've both discovered that he can be a real trial, can't he?"

Relieved, Desha nodded. "He's just so—so impossible," she said, her voice rising agitatedly. "Why, one minute he's absolutely irresistibly attractive, and the next minute he's treating me like I couldn't find my way out of a paper bag."

She bit her lip. She hadn't wanted to come here and talk about Bryce. Elayne had said they were going to discuss the shop. She met the other woman's interested eyes. "I'm sorry. I don't want to talk about Bryce. You invited me to lunch to talk about the store. Now if you want to let me go, I assure you I'll understand perfectly, and there'll be no hard feelings."

"Let you go?" Elayne repeated. "Why, my dear girl, I'm hoping you'll buy the shop from me."

Too taken aback to speak, Desha stared uncomprehendingly at the other woman. Surely Elayne wasn't serious!

Chapter Eight

Desha's moment of nearly unequaled excitement disappeared as quickly as it had come. The light dying in her eyes, she murmured, "Did Bryce put you up to this? Is this some attempt of his at setting my feet on the proper path, of giving me the unparalleled charitable assist?"

"Bryce!" Elayne cried. "You discredit me, Desha! Of course it wasn't Bryce's idea. He has no notion I'm here or what I'm going to propose to you. *I* own that shop. *I* determine what becomes of it—and the other one I own."

"I'm sorry," Desha murmured. Of course Bryce hadn't initiated this. He had washed his hands of her last night. And, anyway, she couldn't afford to buy *Southern Elegance & not so elegants*. The whole idea was preposterous.

"Well, no need to be sorry," Elayne said. "I'm sure this is a total surprise to you, but I've been thinking about it since I saw your enthusiasm at the shop the day I came in.''

She took a sip of her tea, then set the glass down and leaned forward. "Desha, I'm sixty-one years old. I've put all the years of my adult work life into that shop. I've put my very heart into it—at least the parts that weren't given to my husband or my son. It came third only to them. But now I'm ready to retire.''

Smiling, she settled back into her chair. "Stephen and I have plans to travel, to spend some of that money—and the money he has from the tire business he recently sold. Since you've met Stephen, I'm sure you can understand that I no longer have the time or the energy necessary to run a business, especially a clothing business that demands close attention. I want to devote my time to him now,'' she said with a wry smile.

"Yes, of course I can understand,'' Desha said. "He's delightful.''

"Thank you. I think so, as you've already guessed,'' Elayne said playfully. "However, it has always torn me apart to think of abandoning to just anyone the business into which I put so much of myself. The second shop, *Southern Pride*, isn't critical to me. It was simply a prudent business investment, but I dreamed and cried and sweated over *Southern Elegance*. Frankly, I simply couldn't bear to consider giving it up until I saw you at work that day.''

"I'm sorry, Elayne,'' Desha interrupted, "but I've already explained to you that I have no money. I couldn't possibly buy the business.''

"Don't you want it?''

"Yes! Of course I want it! It's my dream! But that's not the determining factor, is it? I just can't afford it.''

"I'm surprised at you," the older woman said with a mock-stern face. "Where's that optimism? What about fate? What about your horoscope?"

Desha smiled. "If fate were on my side in this, I would have the money to buy the business."

"Not true," Elayne disputed. "If fate hadn't sent you to the shop, I wouldn't be here making this offer, and if fate hadn't decreed that it be so, I wouldn't be in the position of telling you that I want to make you the controlling working partner."

"But—" Desha began.

"Just listen," Elayne insisted. "You can do what you want with *Southern Elegance & not so elegants*, as long as you can make payments to me for the shop. You will, of course, be in charge of both shops. I think the customers expect the same selections at both stores. And if you increase profits, you actually double your money since you'll have two stores. And when you show enough profit, you simply buy me out. What could be easier?"

What could be easier indeed? Desha wondered. Could it be that simple? Could it be fate? Could her dream possibly be right at her fingertips? No, it was too easy.

"I'm sorry, but I can't do it," she murmured, her voice heavy with disappointment.

"But why?"

"I—it—it sounds like charity to me. It would go against my principles."

"Charity!" Elayne whispered the word as if it were scandalous. "Why, Desha Smith, now I see that there's a side to Bryce's story, too. Where on earth do you get charity from in this situation, my dear girl? I need to sell my shop. No, I *have* to sell my shop because I cannot devote the time to it any longer. Now it's true that I could have Bryce continue to oversee it just as he has been doing. And I could also watch it go right down the drain for lack of interested on-the-premises management."

She waved a hand. "Not that Bernice and Mira haven't tried, but *Southern Elegance & not so elegants* is an out-of-the-ordinary shop. Someone has to run it who *feels* the pulse of the shop as though it were a real entity, not just a room with some clothes."

"I do know what you mean," Desha agreed passionately. "I understand precisely." She had felt that way about her shop.

"Of course," Elayne said, "Bernice has worked for me for years. I would hate to see her lose her job, but you do have final say."

"Oh, I get along fine with Bernice," Desha said. "I wouldn't dream of dismissing her from *Southern Pride*."

Elayne settled back more contentedly. "Now, I know you and Bryce have your differences," she said gently, "but could you possibly put them aside long enough to discuss this with him?"

Bryce, Desha thought to herself. Of course he would play some role in this, but Elayne continued before she could even try to explain how awkward it would be to talk to Bryce.

"He will, of course, be overseeing the legal end. I long ago turned all that over to him. I don't even know enough about particulars to work with you on it. I do know, as you should be aware, that we've been losing money for the last two quarters."

"But that's no problem, believe me," Desha insisted. "I'm already showing a profit, and just the other day I had an idea—'' Her voice trailed off and she shrugged in embarrassment. "Well, I had thought of some other ways to increase business, with your permission, of course."

Elayne attempted not to look too pleased. "Then you will consider buying the shop?"

There was a tense pause while Desha tried not to pinch herself to see if she was awake. Maybe it was fate, and if it was, did she intend to let the chance of a lifetime slip away? Wouldn't she be a fool not to see if the star at hand was really meant for her? After all, she *knew* she could succeed. She recalled thinking that before she painted the shop.

The decision was immediate. "Consider it?" she murmured excitedly, the dream at her fingertips causing her to rush forward recklessly. "There's nothing to consider. I'd love the shop, and I can't tell you how grateful I am for this opportunity."

Her mind was racing faster than her tongue now. "You won't be sorry for your confidence in me, I promise you. Why I'll have that shop in the black in no time. In fact, I'll have it paid off before—'' She sat back in her chair and laughed. "I'm afraid I'm getting carried away. Forgive me."

"Please don't apologize. That's why we're here. I love your enthusiasm. That's what the shop needs," Elayne said, reaching across to take Desha's hands in hers. Her large diamond ring caught on the table cloth.

"Oh dear," she said as she loosened the threads that had been snagged. "Sometimes this ring is a hazard."

"It's very, very beautiful," Desha said, watching the diamonds sparkle as Elayne worked the ring free.

Their eyes met. "Thank you," Elayne said softly. "it was my first husband's mother's ring. It will belong to Bryce's bride one day."

For a moment Desha simply couldn't look away. Bryce's bride. Why did those words hurt so much? Why did the thought of Bryce hurt so much? Why couldn't she just stay angry with him?

Elayne freed the ring and squeezed Desha's fingers. "Thank you. You've made my life so much simpler today. Now let's eat our lunch so I can hurry home and tell Stephen. He'll be so pleased."

"Yes, of course," Desha said, reaching for her fork again.

Somehow the mention of Bryce's bride had taken the wind from her sails. She was as eager as Elayne to leave the restaurant.

When Norman had dropped her off at the shop, she hurried inside as if the devil himself were chasing her. It wasn't until she was totally lost in both her work and the incredible idea that she might actually own the shop one day, that she could forget about Bryce, even momentarily.

When Bryce arrived at his mother's house that evening, he found her in a wonderful mood. In fact, he told himself warily, she looked like the cat who'd swallowed the canary.

"Bryce, darling, how good of you to join me and Stephen on such short notice," she exclaimed, embracing him warmly.

"Mother," he said without preliminaries, "what's this all about? What have you been up to?"

"Why, Bryce," she said in a mock-hurt tone, "whatever do you mean?"

"I know you," he returned. "You've got something on your mind besides a simple dinner at home. What is it?"

"Of course I have something on my mind, Son," she answered honestly, giving him a warm smile. "But, for heaven's sake, let's follow some rules of polite society. Have a drink. We'll discuss what's on my mind over dinner."

When she noticed Bryce tightening his lips, she leaned over and kissed him, then turned to her husband. "Stephen, will you please get the drinks?"

Half an hour later, while they ate succulent roast beef and scalloped potatoes, Elayne told an amazed Bryce of her plans. "Now, of course I want you to oversee the transaction," she said sweetly. "You've always been personally involved in the shop."

"Mother, I will not oversee the transaction," he returned sharply. "You know how Desha and I feel about each other, and anyway, I certainly don't think this is a sound business venture. It's hardly proper."

"Proper?" she repeated. "That shop is my heart, you know that, Bryce. Proper isn't even a consideration. And, yes, I do know how you and Desha feel about each other." She gave him one of her most charming smiles. "I need you to handle this, because it is out of the ordinary."

"I want no part of it," he said firmly. "And don't you think you're acting rather hastily?"

Elayne shook her head. "No, I don't. I've considered selling the shop for some time. The idea became more viable the day Desha phoned and wanted to know if she could make some changes there. The notion of selling firmed in my mind when I saw her changes, her enthusiasm, her zest."

Bryce pressed his lips into a thin line. He didn't believe he was hearing this. How could Desha step into their lives right off the street and turn them upside down? How was it possible that she had become so involved with them?

"Bryce, please help a fellow out," Stephen put in earnestly. "Your mother is finally willing to sever the strings to that shop. It means she and I will be free to live our lives as we see fit. I'd take it as a great favor if you would personally handle just this one transaction for her. How about it?"

Bryce rolled his eyes and sighed tiredly. Ever since Desha had come into his life, he had been thrown out of kilter every way he turned. How could his mother ask him to do this? Stephen, who didn't know the particulars, could be forgiven, but not his mother.

"The lawyers can handle it perfectly well, foolish though they'll think it is," Bryce insisted. "You don't need me for this."

Elayne looked at Stephen with a hurt expression on her face. "Bryce has always had a hand in *Southern Elegance*. Perhaps I did use my heart instead of my head. Maybe this isn't a good idea."

She stared at the silverware, pensively tracing a fork handle. "Naturally, I want Desha to buy the other shop, too, if this goes well. I don't have the personal interest in that one I have in this one, and there's no point in hanging on to either of them if Desha can take over, but maybe Bryce is right." She made a tsking sound. "Desha will be so disappointed."

"I don't know why," Bryce said. "I'm surprised that she considered it at all. I should think it would smack of charity to her."

"Oh, it did, at first," Elayne said.

"That figures," Bryce muttered.

"But her horoscope had mentioned a new business opportunity today," Elayne continued, "and, after all, owning her own shop again has been her dream. I want to sell the shop to someone who will care about it, so everything seemed so perfect. She and I determined that it had to be fate."

"Fate," Bryce said with a groan. "Mother, I don't believe you said that."

"And why not?" she countered. "In truth, how can you deny all the coincidences? Desha just happened to break down where you were; we needed a new clerk; she had had prior experience; she immediately became intensely involved in the shop." She carefully and deliberately avoided mentioning the spark between Desha and Bryce. "Don't *you* think it might be fate, Bryce?"

He didn't think anything of the kind, but he could imagine Desha believing that it was. He felt a tightness in his chest as he imagined how excited she might be at the prospect of owning the shop. It was her dream.

A dream, he reluctantly admitted, that he would give to her himself if it were in his power. And apparently it was, no matter how unsound it might be as far as business was concerned. He sighed. If this was what Elayne and Desha wanted, who was he to object?

"All right, Mother," he said in a resigned voice. "You win. I'll handle the transaction."

Two days later, Desha was startled when Bryce walked into the shop without any warning, not even a phone call. Bracing herself for a confrontation, she folded her arms and waited for him to approach the counter.

She was aware that her heart was beating wildly, and although she told herself that it was because Bryce was going to handle the shop transfer with her, she also knew that it was partly because he was here at all. She was alarmed by the weakness she felt inside. Why did she have to react to this man so fervently?

"Good morning," he said, startling her from her thoughts.

"Good morning," she returned, her voice guarded. This was the first time they had seen each other since the night they quarreled. She didn't know how to react.

Bryce reminded himself that he had vowed to stick strictly to business, but the vow wasn't easy to keep now that he was here in front of this woman who inexplicably stirred his very soul. His desire for her was almost self-destructive in view of the way she felt about him. Why couldn't he just get this over with and go about his business? Why did he have the urge to attempt all over again to explain the way he felt to her?

He gazed at her, trying to think of how to begin a business discussion when all he could think of was the woman. His pulse began to pound at his temples. He couldn't take his eyes off her. He seemed intent on savoring every detail of the bright outfit she wore, the way the pink gave her cheeks color, and matched the lipstick so perfectly on those tantalizing lips. What was the matter with him anyway?

It was a stupid question, because he knew perfectly well what was wrong. He was in love with Desha. He couldn't even look at her without knowing it for a fact. That was why he had agreed to handle the shop transaction. It gave him another chance with Desha, another opportunity to see if they had a future together. Damn Cupid! He had made a ridiculous error with his arrow. He had missed the mark by a mile. Somehow he had pierced Bryce's heart.

"I believe Mrs. Hammond sent you to discuss my purchasing the store," Desha said, unable to bear the suspense any longer. That was why he was here, wasn't it? And why did she feel so foolish when she asked? It all seemed like such a dream, an impossible dream, just like her dreams of the man. She wanted to run into his arms. She wanted to plead with him to forget business and talk about them. She wanted to. But, of course, she didn't.

"Yes," Bryce said, clearing his throat and apologizing. Of course all Desha wanted to discuss was business. "We need to arrange a time for you to see the books and to meet with our lawyers. We need to work out some reasonable payments, which will, of course, have to be figured on your projected profits. You need to give careful consideration to such facts before we put them down on paper and finalize them at the lawyers' office."

"Yes, I understand that," she said. Actually, it was all she had been thinking about—when she wasn't thinking of Bryce. "I have the figures I believe I can work with, if they're agreeable to you," she said, pulling some sheets of paper from beneath the counter and coming around to the other side where he stood.

Bryce was having an awful time concentrating. The only figure on his mind was hers. Why did she look more beautiful today than he had ever seen her? He felt even more vulnerable to her charms now that the counter no longer acted as a barrier. He smelled the faint scent of her perfume as she approached him.

"Excellent," he said, and was surprised by the hoarseness of his voice. "I'll take these with me. When I've reviewed them, and you've seen the books, we'll discuss viable options—say on Thursday?"

"Will it be possible to do it after work?" she asked. "I don't want to lose any business time."

Bryce resisted the urge to shake his head. She was going to go about this the way she did everything, passionately, and without restraint.

"I think you could close the shop for a few hours, couldn't you? Or maybe you should think of hiring someone. You can't spend every waking hour here, you know."

"Oh, but I can," she insisted. "Other than the few hours Bernice comes in, I've been doing all the work by myself, and now I'll have even more dedication. Until, of course," she added, "the business prospers enough so that I'll *have* to hire additional help."

Bryce couldn't contain a grin. Wasn't it just like the irrepressible Desha to already be thinking of needing someone else because of business expanding so much?

"How about Sunday?" he said. "Could we do it on Sunday? You will close the shop then, won't you?"

She smiled sheepishly. "Yes. The only thing I had planned for Sunday was a bus tour of the area—I need to get my bearings, find my way around. As soon as Betty is repaired, I've got to check out my competition."

Bryce resisted the impulse to shake his head in dismay. In the two days since his mother had proposed this plan, Desha had raced full-speed ahead, determined to pull this off, to make a success of *Southern*

Elegance & not so elegants. He didn't know why it should amaze him; it was typical Desha. She had been thinking about business while he had been brooding about her, about them.

"I'll take you around the city, if you'd like," he offered. "Strictly business," he qualified when he saw her strained expression. "I know where the competition is. We can kill two birds with one stone. We'll review the books, discuss payments, and decide when to meet with the lawyers to finalize the transaction."

Even though Desha knew it wasn't good for her heart to spend any more time with Bryce than she had to, this made sense from a business standpoint.

"Thank you. I would appreciate that—if it's not too much trouble, and if you don't mind being seen with colorful me."

Oh, shucks! she told herself as she watched his smile fade. Why hadn't she been content with a simple thank you? Why did she always speak before she thought? The man was trying to help, even if his interest was only in the business, and she had responded unprofessionally.

Bryce drew in a steadying breath and told himself that she wasn't going to roil him that easily this morning. Before he could respond, she murmured, "I'm sorry. I shouldn't have said that."

A slow smile played on his lips as he watched her contrite expression, the big brown eyes soft and apologetic, the pretty mouth trembling slightly.

"No harm done," he said softly. "Will nine be too early? We could go to breakfast. I like to start the day with a full stomach."

She nodded. "Nine will be fine, thank you."

"I'll pick you up at the hotel."

"All right."

Desha watched as he turned and walked to the door. She couldn't look away until he had vanished from her sight. Only after the door was closed and Bryce was nowhere to be seen did she let herself inhale deeply, trying her best to still her trembling insides. She had been a fool to agree to spend time with him, but what choice did she have?

Desha couldn't decide if Sunday came too swiftly, or if the time had dragged interminably. She had thrown herself totally into the business, her mind spinning with thoughts and plans, but throughout it all, there had been Bryce, ever-present, ever-tormenting, ever in the midst of all her dreams—there, but unachievable, a dream never to be realized, no matter how she planned and schemed, a man fate had set apart from her.

She started when two sharp raps sounded on the door. Drawing in a steadying breath, she smoothed a baggy red and white blouse down over fitted ankle-length blue denim slacks. An elastic blue belt and blue flats completed the outfit. She felt ridiculously like she was going on a date with the man, instead of joining him to discuss business. She had wanted to look casual, but attractive.

"Good morning," Bryce said warmly. His gaze skimmed down her attire. "You look very patriotic," he noted, not adding that the form-fitting jeans hugged her figure enticingly and the red set off her dark eyes and hair most appealingly.

"Is that a compliment?" she asked, determined not to take offense at every turn and speak in haste.

He grinned. "As close as I dare to come, I believe."

"Then I'll say thank you."

For a moment those hypnotic blue eyes of his held her captive. She found that she could only lower her gaze the merest fraction, and then she focused on his lips, those deliciously kissable lips. She made herself look lower, thinking that his conservative clothing would jar her sluggish brain, but the blue shirt only emphasized his masculinity. Open at the neck, it revealed the dark curling hair on his chest. Finally, she forced herself to reach for her purse.

"I'm ready when you are," she said brightly.

"Fine. I'm starving."

To Desha's surprise, Bryce took her to one of the fast-food restaurants just down the street from the hotel. For a moment she sat in the car too incredulous to even open her own door. Bryce walked around and opened it.

"Are we eating here?" she asked.

He laughed. "I fooled you, didn't I? You thought we were going to some stuffy restaurant. Well, I decided to get off my narrow path today. I want to have an egg on a biscuit, and coffee in a Styrofoam cup."

"You're not serious?"

"I am," he insisted with a big smile. "I know you eat here often. I want to see what's so appealing."

Laughing openly, Desha walked with Bryce into the crowded restaurant. She began to relax a little. He was really trying to make this easy for her. Maybe she could get through the day after all. Maybe . . .

Chapter Nine

After they had eaten breakfast, Bryce took Desha to his business office where Judy, the bookkeeper, went over records with them. Desha wasn't deterred by the previous steady decline in profits, and, after considerable debate, she and Bryce were able to work out what she felt was a more than equitable arrangement for her buying *Southern Elegance & not so elegants*, and eventually *Southern Pride*. A date was decided upon to discuss the final arrangements with the lawyers.

"I think that's about it," Bryce finally noted.

Desha looked up from the paperwork, sorry that the business discussion was at an end. She had admired Bryce's business acumen tremendously and she was impressed by his strategy for transferring the business in such a manner that benefited both his mother and her.

"I believe so," she said reluctantly, left with no other option.

Bryce glanced down at his watch. "Can you believe it's after noon? No wonder I'm hungry. How about a bite of lunch?"

"I'd like that," Desha agreed more quickly than she felt she should have. Business was one thing; pleasure quite another. A few hours with Bryce, and she would be dreaming the impossible again.

"Good," he said with a winning smile. "Business discussions always make me hungry. How about seafood?"

"Sounds wonderful. I've been meaning to try some of the Virginia Beach seafood. I'm told it's excellent," she said.

"Indeed, it is. I'll take you to one of my favorite restaurants right on the water."

Desha's brown eyes glowed. "Great. I love the water."

"Judy, will you file this paperwork for us, please?" Bryce asked, turning to the bookkeeper. "And make an appointment with Welsh and Carpp to do the contract."

Judy agreed with a warm smile, and Bryce and Desha headed for the restaurant.

"Oh, a lighthouse!" she exclaimed when they approached the charming restaurant.

"Apparently you like lighthouses," Bryce said.

"I'm especially fascinated by them!" she exclaimed.

Bryce smiled and told himself that she was no doubt especially fascinated by just about everything—at least briefly.

"Have you been to the Old Cape Henry Lighthouse?" he asked.

"No, but I read about it."

He waved a hand. "Reading about it hardly compares to experiencing it. I'll take you there after lunch. It's near one of the most popular clothing shops in the city, so it won't be out of our way. I want to see how much stamina you have. If you can walk up all those winding stairs to the top window, the view is incredible."

"I can do it!" she returned, having no idea how many steps were involved. She wasn't about to pass up such a challenge, especially from Bryce Gerrard.

"We'll see," he said with a grin. "We'll see."

Lunch more than lived up to Desha's expectations. In a delightful dining room decorated with nautical memorabilia, she and Bryce sampled a delicious variety of seafood, including shrimp, crab and clams.

"I'm stuffed," she declared at last. "And I think I just gained five pounds."

Bryce grinned at her. "Don't worry. You'll lose every ounce of it when you climb to the top of the lighthouse—if you climb to the top."

Brown eyes glowing, she challenged, "Bet I can go farther than you."

He laughed. "Clearly you don't realize how many steps there are, Desha."

"It doesn't matter," she insisted recklessly. "I can do it."

His blue eyes twinkled. "I believe you just might do it. Indestructible Desha. That's what your mother should have named you."

"Oh, believe me, I'm not indestructible," she murmured, remembering how she had cried all night long after the pool party. No, she wasn't indestructible at all. Not when it came to this man.

"No?" he murmured thoughtfully.

"No. Well," she said with a sigh, some of the fun of the anticipated lighthouse climb vanishing as she recalled that tearful night, "we should get under way, shouldn't we, if we're going to see the lighthouse and my shop competition." She glanced at the big face of her wristwatch. "It's almost two o'clock."

A short time later Desha's eyes widened as she and Bryce drove through the gate to Fort Story. Nestled in thick greenery, the old brick lighthouse pierced the clear blue sky, high over the ocean.

"It's very tall," she said, awed by the structure.

"That it is," Bryce agreed. "Towering and magnificent. Did you read that it was commissioned by President George Washington and authorized and funded by America's first Congress?"

"No, I didn't. I did read that it was built in 1791 to warn mariners entering the Virginia Capes and that it's the official symbol of the city and a registered National Historical Landmark."

"Let's show it to you then," he said.

Desha waited while he paid the small admission fee, then headed with him up the many steps leading to the lighthouse. Much to her chagrin, she was breathing hard before they even reached the building itself.

"Tired?" Bryce murmured when she paused at the top of the steps.

Embarrassed, she shook her head. "No, I'm just feeling the effects of carrying around all the food we ate for lunch."

Bryce smiled, but he didn't contradict her. Taking her hand in his, he guided her to the lighthouse door.

Desha told herself that the shivers up and down her spine were from the anticipation of climbing up in the lighthouse, but she couldn't be positive they weren't caused by Bryce's touch. When they entered the brick tower, she looked up, staring wide-eyed at the winding steps leading up and up and up toward the top.

"Oh, Bryce," she whispered. "I had no idea."

"I didn't think so. Is the bet still on?" he teased.

"Of course," she said with typical Aries defiance. She would do it, she promised herself, even if it killed her. And it just might.

She savored the warm pressure of Bryce's fingers around hers as he preceded her up the spiraling stairs. They were the only people inside at the moment, and their footsteps echoed on the steps as they wound 'round and 'round until they reached the first window and stopped to peer out.

Desha hoped Bryce didn't hear the rapid beating of her heart. She couldn't quite decide why it pounded so fiercely. She told herself that the physical exertion was so much more than she had imagined, but she wasn't sure the wild beat hadn't been going on ever since Bryce stepped into that shop that morning. She was acutely aware of his warm hand still holding hers, of his overpowering presence as he stood inches from her in the confining space, pointing out sights from the window.

"Ready?" he asked, and Desha realized that she had been staring at his blue eyes instead of the ocean.

"Ready when you are."

He chuckled as he started up the stairs again. Up and up they went, and the higher they climbed, the more Desha began to submerge herself in the splendor of the old lighthouse. She wondered about the tales it could tell about time and men.

Bryce paused on the step above her and looked back down. "How are you doing?"

"Fine," she returned breathlessly. "It really is magnificent. I wonder who the men were that built it in 1791. Did they have families who came to marvel at it? And who manned it? Who came out on the dark and dreary nights to work the lights? And what about the sailors who sailed the seas? Did they heave a tremendous sigh of relief when the lighthouse came into view on a turbulent night? And what were their lives like? I wonder what it was like to live two hundred years ago."

Bryce smiled and shook his head as she paused to draw a deep breath. "We can go to Lynnhaven House and you can see how they lived years ago if you're interested," he told her. "It was constructed between 1725 and 1730, and it's one of the best-preserved 18th century middle-class homes in America."

"Oh, I do want to see that!" she cried.

"Somehow I thought you might," he murmured, "but on the other hand, you strike me as a thoroughly-modern-Milly, so I wasn't sure."

"Now that I've seen the lighthouse, I'm hungry for more of Virginia's history," she exclaimed. "My mind is whirling with thoughts and questions."

"Tell me," he said very seriously, "do you always get so caught up in *everything*?"

She grinned. "Yes, I'm afraid that I do. An Aries, you know."

Yes, he told himself, he was beginning to know. He had never met anyone quite like this woman. Being with her was an adventure in itself. He didn't know when or what she would do next. Or where or how long she would be involved in it.

The thought unsettled him. "Ready to move on?" he asked abruptly.

When she nodded, he clasped her hand more tightly and began the upward trek again. The short pause had helped him catch his breath, and Desha seemed to be going full speed ahead mentally as well as physically. He could sense the excitement, the tension pulsing through her as she held his hand tightly.

Lost in her thoughts, she pondered the pride behind the preservation of the lighthouse. She had been too much of a wanderer, too busy rushing on to the next place, the next dream, to pay much attention to tradition, but she could understand the pride the Virginians took in their Southern heritage. She had a glimpse of the reasoning behind the name *Southern Elegance* and *Southern Pride*, and again that feeling that she belonged here, that she could be a part of this, swept over her.

They stopped to study the view from another window before they reached their final destination, the third window, and there Desha experienced the most thrilling moment of all. From their vantage point near the top of the tower, they were able to see much of the surrounding area and the endless blue expanse of sea.

"Oh, Bryce, it's stunning!" she cried, turning to look at him, her heart fluttering, her eyes bright.

Impulsively, he gathered her close, holding her against his heart, wanting to savor the fire in her soul, the spirit that soared as high as the lighthouse.

Her pulse racing, Desha wrapped her arms around Bryce and clung tightly, waiting for the beating of her heart to slow, but it didn't happen. She felt giddy and light-headed, and she couldn't attribute it all to the height of the third window. She felt sure that Bryce was going to kiss her, and she wanted his kiss very much.

The sound of other visitors coming up the steps drove the couple apart. Bryce looked as dazed as Desha when she gazed into his face.

He seemed reluctant to move for a moment, then he murmured, "We'd better go back down if you want to see Lynnhaven House and your clothing competition today."

After all, they were together today ostensibly for the purposes of business. He wanted to go very slowly with this woman this time. He didn't want to rush a relationship with her. He wanted to feel his way, to pace their time so that neither of them shied away before they had a chance to get past the extremes in their personalities—the bull and the ram, she had spoken of.

"Yes," she said, the word sounding so husky that it embarrassed her. "Yes," she tried again, clearing her throat, "I think so."

Yet she didn't know if she could go back down all those steps. She felt as if she could only lift higher and higher, from sheer elation at Bryce's touch.

On the stairs, they passed other people and had to make way for them, but Desha hardly noticed. She had intended to count the steps on the way back, but now all she could think of was Bryce and how much she wanted to be in his arms again. She was still in a fog when they returned to the car.

"The shop that provides the most competition for you is just down the street," Bryce said.

Desha blinked, trying to concentrate on what he was saying. "Just down the street," she parroted, attempting to make her brain function.

"Yes," he said. In minutes, he had stopped in front of the building. "It's not as established as *Southern Elegance & not so elegants*, but it does an excellent year-round business."

"Oh, I'm not worried about not having a good business year round," she told him confidently, finally able to focus on the subject at hand. "I've got my strategy all mapped out."

A small frown creased her forehead. "In fact," she said, her mind spinning, "I'm thinking of adding yet another facet to the store—or maybe I'll wait until I buy into the second store. While I was in the lighthouse, it occurred to me that with Virginians so proud of their Southern heritage, I think I can successfully carry scarves and shawls copied from the Colonial period. I can use them as dramatic accessories for my existing stock, and, of course, I want them made right here in Virginia."

Before Bryce could comment, she added, "And, they'll make wonderful souvenirs for the traveler on a budget." She glanced at him. "I don't have to tell you that tourism is big business in Virginia Beach."

Staring at her in amazement, Bryce could only nod. Did every single experience, every occurrence send her spinning? But he had to admit that he thought the scarf idea was an excellent one, just the kind of thing an entrepreneur like Desha might think of.

Funny that he had used the word "entrepreneur." When he first met her, he didn't think she could successfully carry off being a sales clerk. Now he was truly beginning to believe that she could make a success of his mother's stores.

She was already climbing out of the car to get a better look at her competition when Bryce sat staring at her, watching the way her jeans outlined her shapely legs and derriere, the way her dark hair glistened in the sun.

Suddenly she motioned madly to him. "Come look, Bryce!" she called excitedly.

Wondering what she had discovered, he went to stand beside her as she peered into the window. "They've enlivened their walls too. I wonder if they saw mine?"

Frowning, Bryce cupped his hands before his eyes so that he could see into the store more clearly. There, bold and bright and as big as life, was a wall full of colorfully painted circles with clothes in their centers.

In truth, Bryce had never seen this store do anything so dramatic, but he wasn't sure it wasn't merely coincidence. "It does seem that you two had the same idea," he said.

"Yes," she murmured thoughtfully, "and it also means that they *are* competition for me. They must be on my same wavelength. Well, I'll just have to work that much harder."

"I think you'll be just fine," Bryce said, facing her.

"Do you really?" she murmured, wanting him to believe in her, needing him to be proud of her.

For a long moment, they gazed at each other, unable to look away. As his eyes searched her face, her animated features, it was all Bruce could do to keep from kissing her.

"Yes, I do," he said at last, his voice husky.

"Thank you, Bryce." Desha still looked at him. Her heart had begun to beat erratically in anticipation of another of his kisses.

The moment seemed to stretch interminably, until Bryce spoke, shattering it. "We'd better head toward Lynnhaven House. I think they close around four or five."

She glanced at her watch, embarrassed because she had been so sure he would kiss her, and he hadn't. "Yes, we need to hurry," she agreed, already rushing toward the car.

Bryce shook his head as he watched her spin away, her short hair dancing in the breeze she was creating in her haste. And he wondered if it were possible for any man to catch the wind, or tame a woman like Desha Smith.

Desha was enthralled by Lynnhaven House, which was almost three hundred years old. The knowledgeable, costumed guide showed them from room to room, each one decorated with period furniture, and informed them of life as it had been when the occupants of the house had lived there.

When they were shown a baby's handmade cradle and durable clothes, the guide excused herself for a moment. As Desha glanced at Bryce, she couldn't help but wonder what it would be like to hold a child of his in her arms, to have children and grandchildren to carry the name Gerrard through the years, to leave a legacy of love and baby dresses and memories.

She studied the structure of the crib, then stared at the baby clothes. She started when Bryce spoke; she hadn't realized until then that she was tracing the pattern of the small baby garment. She quickly withdrew her hand.

"Don't tell me you want to stock baby clothes in the shop now?" Bryce had been watching the way she had touched the baby garment. His thoughts had suddenly been full of the grandchildren his mother wanted so fervently, grandchildren with Desha's spirit. But, of course, Desha had been thinking only of business.

Looking up at him, she smiled. She wondered what he would say if she told him the only baby clothes she was thinking of were the ones a child of theirs might wear.

"You aren't seriously thinking of stocking baby clothes," he said when she didn't speak.

She shook her head. "That wasn't what I was thinking, Bryce."

"No?" he murmured. "And just what was going through that pretty head of yours?" The way she looked at him, he dared, for just a moment, to think it had something to do with him.

Desha glanced back over her shoulder when the guide reappeared.

"Sorry for the delay," the woman said, quickly explaining what had happened. "Ready?"

Bryce felt a moment of disappointment as he and Desha left the child's room. He wished the guide had delayed just a little longer. But she hadn't and that was that.

When the house tour was completed, they were shown the garden and the cemetery. Then it was time to leave.

"You might enjoy seeing my house," Bryce noted when they returned to the car. "It's almost a hundred years old, although much of it has been renovated. The cottage I told you about is nearly in its original state."

Desha didn't know what to say. Was he inviting her to show her an interesting house, or was there more to it? Before she could dare to dream, Bryce continued.

"How about dinner on Friday night? I'll invite Elayne and Stephen if you'd like."

Desha tried to smother a surge of disappointment. Truthfully, she would have preferred the evening alone with him, but she didn't dare say so. Surely it was best that Elayne and Stephen come.

Maybe Bryce honestly had no more interest in her now than their business tie; after all, he had made it perfectly clear what he thought about her, hadn't he?

"Dinner sounds nice," she murmured. "It will be good to see Elayne and Stephen again."

By Wednesday, Friday evening seemed like a long time away. Desha had been very busy with the shop and her plans, but time dragged. She knew that it was because she couldn't stop thinking about Bryce, no matter how fiercely she applied herself to her tasks. When the phone rang at four, she jumped.

"Hello," she said, forcing herself to sound bright and cheerful.

"Hello," Elayne said. "How are you?"

"Fine," Desha said politely. "Fine, and very busy, I'm happy to say. And you?"

"Oh, I'm just wonderful now that I've finally been able to find someone who will love my business. Bryce told me he and you had worked everything out. He says you have more ideas to increase profits."

Desha laughed. "Yes, more ideas than I have time and money."

"I'd just love to hear about them," Elayne exclaimed enthusiastically. "Are you free tonight? May

I extend a spur-of-the-moment invitation to a simple supper at the house?''

Desha was delighted that Elayne wanted to hear her ideas. It was good to have someone with an interest in them eager to listen. "I'd love to come by, but I'm afraid I'll have to miss supper. I have to work late tonight.''

"How late?''

"I'm not sure. Perhaps until after seven.''

"That's fine. I'll have Norman pick you up—say about seven-thirty.''

"Only if you don't hold supper for me,'' Desha insisted, knowing that many Southerners ate early evening meals. "I'll have a quick sandwich at the place on the corner.''

"Nonsense,'' Elayne said. "We'll all eat at seven-thirty. It's not that much later than usual for us anyway.''

"All right,'' Desha agreed, welcoming the thought of a good meal and Elayne and Stephen's refreshing company. "See you then.''

By seven-thirty, she was still knee-deep in planning her scarf and shawl line, but she grabbed her purse, locked the shop door and rushed out to meet Norman who had already pulled up to the curb.

In minutes she was whisked over to Elayne's lovely home. She smiled as Elayne, dressed in another caftan, came out on the porch to greet her.

"You look beautiful,'' she told the older woman.

"Do you really like this?'' Elayne asked. "I ordered a line of them as you and I discussed. They should be arriving soon.''

"Great!'' Desha cried. "They'll be just the thing to go with my new scarf line.''

"Scarf line?" Elayne murmured, her blue eyes glowing. "Come on in and tell me all about it!"

Over dinner, the two women chattered so incessantly about Desha's plans that Stephen barely had a chance to get in a word.

When the doorbell rang, he hopped up eagerly. "At last! Male companionship!" he cried. "Bryce is finally here."

"Bryce?" Desha murmured, her heart instantly beginning its irregular rhythm.

"Yes, didn't I tell you?" Elayne asked, her voice casual, but Desha noted that the other woman was avoiding her eyes.

"No."

"Oh, I must have forgotten," Elayne said, rising as Bryce walked into the room.

He stopped abruptly, his gaze meeting Desha's. "I didn't know you had a guest, Mother," he said, never taking his eyes off the younger woman.

"No?" Elayne murmured. "How careless of me to forget to tell you Desha was coming. I must be getting senile."

"Mother," Bryce groaned, but it was plain to see that he wasn't disappointed at all by the unexpected guest. "Good evening, Desha," he said warmly. "And how are you tonight?"

"Fine," she said with equal warmth. And she was. Now that Bryce was here. Quite fine, and looking forward to an even more interesting evening than she had anticipated.

Chapter Ten

Sit down, Son. You're just in time for coffee," Elayne said, barely containing her delight when she saw that Bryce and Desha were smiling at each other. She indicated the chair between her and the younger woman. "I'm pleased that you both are here tonight." Her eyes met Bryce's as he seated himself. "I don't think I've had a chance to tell you that Stephen and I won't be able to join you two on Friday evening after all."

"When did we—" Stephen began, but Elayne interrupted him.

"Stephen, surely I didn't forget to tell you that I'd accepted a prior engagement and hadn't written it on my calendar?" She laughed softly before he could reply. "Oh, my goodness, I don't know if it's being past sixty or if it's love that has my brain so fuddled."

"Mother," Bryce said in exasperation. She had never been absentminded in her life, and she certainly wasn't now. In fact, she was at her cleverest. It *was* love, *his* love that she had in mind. She wanted him and Desha to spend Friday night alone.

As he studied her smiling face, he wondered if the desire to sell her shop hadn't been part of her overall plan to involve him and Desha. He shook his head; he didn't think even she would go that far. In part, it was her need to sell the shop to someone who would love it. But the other part—

"You will forgive me, won't you, Bryce?" she asked sweetly.

"How can I not?" he asked wryly, his gaze holding hers.

When he saw that she realized he knew what she was about, at least she had enough conscience to glance away. Bryce would have laughed if just he and his mother were there, but as he gave his attention to Desha, he realized that she wouldn't take kindly to anyone manipulating her life, for any reason. If she even suspected that Elayne was conniving ways to throw them together, she would balk.

"Well, I guess that leaves just you and me, Desha," he said. "Ever since Mother married Stephen, she hasn't been able to keep a sane thought in her head. I think she calls it love."

"Or is it only lust?" Stephen asked playfully, raising his brows and wriggling his fingers in a wicked parody.

Bryce and Desha laughed aloud at the surprised expression on Elayne's face. "Oh, really, Stephen, you're making me blush," she said. "Becky," she called, directing her attention to the cook, "will you bring some coffee, please?"

Desha met Bryce's eyes. She felt that old now-familiar shivering sensation as he smiled at her. When she glanced at Elayne and saw the way she was grinning at Stephen, Desha wondered if she would ever know the kind of love the couple shared. Clearly, they adored each other unconditionally. She told herself that was what she wanted when she married.

She looked back at Bryce and saw that he was studying her thoughtfully. She realized that *he* was what she really wanted, and she wondered if he could read her mind, if he knew that she thought about him constantly.

Sighing, she gave her attention to the cup of coffee Becky was pouring for her. She knew she would never find the sweet, playful kind of love with Bryce that Elayne and Stephen shared, but she couldn't deny that Bryce was the most tantalizing man she had ever met. If only he would give a little, let himself open up—

She brushed aside the thought. There she went again, trying to cheat fate, trying to fit Bryce into her Aries life, and knowing that it was like talking to the wind. But when she glanced at him again and found that he was still watching her, she dreamed the impossible—she wanted the impossible.

"I was so relieved when I heard you at the door, Bryce," Stephen said. "These two have talked business until my head is ringing with it. I never heard two women go on so over a shop."

Bryce laughed. "I can believe it. I've heard them both before."

"Well, we've gotten it out of our systems for the night," Elayne insisted, smiling at Desha. "Why don't we take our coffee out on the patio and enjoy the night breeze?"

"A good idea," Stephen echoed, standing up. "Let me take this for you." Balancing his cup in one hand, he reached for his wife's with the other.

"Do be careful, Stephen," Elayne cried. "You've never been any good at that sort of thing."

"Nothing to it," he insisted, and, as Desha and Bryce followed with their own coffee, Stephen managed to get out to the patio with his and Elayne's.

They all laughed when he dropped one of the cups just as he set them down on the patio table. "Heck," he groaned. "And I almost made it."

When Elayne returned with a dishcloth and dustpan and cleaned up the mess, she teased, "I think it's past Stephen's bedtime."

"Oh," he said, grinning wickedly, "I do find that I love to go to bed early these nights."

"Stephen!" Elayne cried, "you're acting just like—like—"

"Like a newlywed," Bryce finished for her, chuckling. He smiled at Desha. "I think that's our cue to leave, don't you?"

"Nonsense," Elayne said. "Don't pay any attention to our teasing. Sit down and have your coffee."

Bryce took a sip of his, then set the cup down. "I really do think it's time we called it a night." He turned to Desha. "I'll drive you back to your hotel."

She realized that she had been hoping he would offer ever since he walked into the house. "That would be nice of you, Bryce," she murmured. "I suspect that Norman has already turned in for the night."

Bryce knew that the chauffeur hadn't gone to bed, since he would be anticipating taking Desha back to her hotel, but he only nodded. "I suspect so."

"Yes, I'm sure he has," Elayne echoed with more conviction than was warranted. "That's so nice of you to take Desha home, Bryce." Obviously delighted by the arrangement, she was no longer suggesting that they stay and finish their coffee.

Bryce fought back soft laughter. If he knew his mother, she was already planning the wedding. Funny, he told himself, as he bade the others good-night, the idea didn't sound bad to him either. Foolish maybe, but not bad at all.

"How's the business going?" he asked when he had assisted Desha into the car.

"Very well," she said enthusiastically. "I can see the results from earlier changes already. We've attracted a regular teenage trade, and that's not all bad, you know."

"No, I'm sure it's not," he said with a laugh before he closed her door.

"My shawl and scarf line is coming right along, too," she said when he got in the car. "And your mother says the caftans should be arriving any day. *Southern Elegance & not so elegants* is attracting customers from every walk of life, and I think that's healthy business."

He grinned at her as, brown eyes glowing, she gestured with her ringed hands in her excitement. Suddenly Bryce reached out and clasped them in his. Their eyes met as he pulled her across the seat. He studied her features, savoring the glowing eyes, small nose, and softly parted lips. Lowering his head, he sampled the sweetness of her mouth, loving the way her lips clung to his, the way she tasted, the way she smelled.

Her heart pounding, Desha wrapped her arms around his neck and held Bryce close to her body.

When his tongue dipped into her mouth, she circled it with her own in a ritual dance.

The kiss deepened as Bryce groaned and drew her even nearer. His hands moved over her back and shoulders as though he couldn't touch her enough. His lips left hers to spill fiery little kisses down her throat.

Arching her head, Desha trembled under the heat of his caresses. She'd never known that love could bring such fire and excitement, such passion and pleasure. The tremors increased as his lips found the curve of her breasts, barely visible over the scoop-neck of her T-shirt dress. His hands sought the thrusting peaks that strained against his shirt and he caressed them lovingly.

Carried away on a crest of pleasure, Desha wasn't aware that she moaned softly at the exquisite assault on her senses. She felt as if she had been abandoned when Bryce abruptly drew back from her.

Running a shaking hand through his hair, he said thickly, "I don't know what gets into me with you. Once I touch you, I forget all the things I'm supposed to remember. We're in the driveway of my mother's house. Norman will be coming out to put the car in the garage. I think we should leave while we still can."

Her mouth dry, her senses spinning, Desha could only nod. She, too, had forgotten where they were. She thought she had transcended time in Bryce's arms, so heavenly was the joy. At least, she told herself, Bryce, too, had been moved enough to forget to be practical. A gentle smile on her lips at the thought, she brushed back her hair and tried to breathe evenly, but she didn't know if that would ever be possible again.

After they had driven off, they were both silent for a few moments before Bryce spoke. "I'd like to take you back to that little club—if you promise you won't run out on me again."

Grinning, Desha told him, "I can't promise, because I don't know what you might say to me."

He laughed. "I don't know either, but what do you say we take a chance?" He was very much afraid that he might say that he loved her, that he wanted to spend his life with her. But he had resolved to go slowly this time. He was going to try to remember that.

Desha had a feeling of déjà vu when they entered the small lounge. The piano player was playing something sweet and sentimental. The room was softly lit. Only about a half-dozen people were there.

"Let's start with a dance," Bryce murmured, before even trying to find a table. "I think we were better off at that point the last time we were here."

Smiling, Desha went into his arms, knowing that she would like nothing better. As the music played, she spun slowly around the small floor, loving the feel of Bryce's body against hers. She didn't want this moment, this night, to ever end.

But finally the music did. "I see a table at the back of the room," Bryce murmured, taking her hand to lead her there.

When they had seated themselves and he had ordered drinks for them, Bryce held Desha's hand to his lips and kissed each finger. A short time before he had promised himself that he was not going to rush a romance with this woman, but it was too late. It had been too late for a long time now.

"I'm crazy about you, Desha," he murmured. "Mad about you. Now listen to me and bear with me if I get something wrong here," he said, his fingers laced in hers. "We need to talk about this, and I didn't do very well last time."

Desha's breath was coming so fast, her pulse racing so hard, that she didn't think she could speak if she wanted to. Bryce had said that he was crazy about her! Was there anything else that mattered? Anything more to say?

"I understand perfectly what you mean with the bull and the ram theory," he continued, "but I don't know or care what sign you are, or what sign I am. You're a woman and I'm a man. I want to follow through on that. I want you to promise me that you'll be patient with me."

He stroked her hand with his thumb. "In case you haven't noticed, I'm working very hard to see your side of life, and while I may not believe in the stars determining our destiny, I'm very much afraid that you hold mine in the palm of your hand."

Reaching out to trace his handsome features with her fingers, Desha tried to curb her own impatience. She was sure this was very difficult for Bryce, Bryce the stubborn, cautious Taurus, caught up in a runaway romance with an Aries.

"Your destiny is very safe in my hands, Bryce," she whispered. "I want to see your side of life, too, as long as you're there." She grinned. "I want to stay in Virginia and become a respectable, successful businesswoman."

She wanted to add that she also wanted to become his wife, but, for once in her life, her blunt tongue wasn't her undoing. She was going to try to do things Bryce's way, slowly and patiently, even if she felt like racing out on the Virginia Beach streets and shouting to the world that he had said he cared for her.

He clasped her hand in his and held it to his lips again. "Did I ever thank Betty for breaking down?" he murmured, causing Desha to laugh.

"I don't think so, but you'll get your chance. She's still broken down."

Bryce smiled as he thought of the perfect present for Desha. He would have Betty repaired; perhaps now she wouldn't cry charity. He would have preferred to buy her a new sports car, but he was afraid that he would be met unfavorably. He was trying to remember that Desha wanted to do everything on her own. With her plans for the shops, she would be able to buy her own sports car in a relatively short time.

When their drinks arrived, they each sipped them silently. After a few minutes, Bryce murmured, "I don't think I can stand much more happiness tonight without exploding. Are you ready to go home?"

Desha nodded. She didn't think she ever wanted to leave him again, but she did like the idea of returning to the hotel now. She wanted to look at herself in the mirror and be sure that all of this wasn't a dream. She was still floating on air when Bryce kissed her and left her at her door, explaining that he dare not come in.

Thursday was a busy day at work, but Desha barely noticed. All she could think of was Bryce. He took precedence over everything else in her life. He was the brightest star in her heaven, the most wonderful dream of all, and she was determined to let love take its course. She hadn't even read her horoscope for fear of finding a contradiction to her happiness.

Friday passed as quickly as Thursday had, and at last Desha found herself back in her room, dressing for dinner with Bryce. She couldn't contain the elation that surged up inside her at the very thought. She wanted to see his house, to see how he lived, to see the man who sent her spinning through the heavens with no thought of what was right and what was wrong in the alignment of the stars.

She was all smiles when Bryce knocked at her door. "Come in," she said cheerfully.

"I'll stop in when I bring you home," he said, smiling at her. "Rosy, my part-time housekeeper, left a roast in the oven. I think it best that we eat it while it's still hot."

He held out his hand to her, and Desha willingly took it. She felt as if she were ten feet tall when she walked by his side. She couldn't explain the surge of joy she felt at his very touch, but she savored it.

When he pulled up into the driveway of his renovated farmhouse a short time later, Desha widened her eyes in surprise. "It's beautiful, Bryce," she murmured. "Not as elaborate as your mother's, but so very beautiful."

Bryce laughed. "I'm glad you like it. I don't want elaborate or contemporary," he explained. "I fell in love with this house when I first saw it. I waited seven years for the people who owned it to finally decide they wanted to retire and move to a smaller place. My nearest neighbor is over there."

He pointed to a house across the way. "That's the Crawfords' house—you remember Lizzie and Calvin."

Desha nodded. She did indeed. Lizzie and Calvin and the blue truck the robber drove.

"Well, come on in," he invited brightly. "Let me show you the house."

Desha was walking by his side when she again spied the blue truck. As though fate had decreed it, it whizzed right down the road—with the robber in it! Desha reacted automatically.

"Bryce, that's him! I know it is!" she declared. "Quick! After him."

Bryce rolled his eyes in dismay. "I don't believe this," he groaned. He really didn't. Not now. Why did she have to start with that robber business again?

"Bryce, I don't have time to argue the merits of what you believe. Please follow that man."

"Desha, stop it," he said. "I thought you understood that the truck you saw was the Crawfords'. Remember? We almost scared them to death last time when we chased after them. The *Crawfords*, Desha. An old man and an old woman. They own the blue truck. Of course you're seeing it again. They live in that house."

"Darn it, Bryce! The Crawfords are not in that truck tonight! I tell you I saw *him* this time. The robber! He's a tall, lanky young man with a hard, sun-lined face. I swear it's true."

"Let's just forget this happened and go in and have a pleasant dinner," he said, his jaw muscle twitching ominously as he tried to keep his temper in check. Why did she have to see the robber tonight?

"He's getting away," she said sharply. "You're standing right here on the porch and letting him ride off to freedom."

Straightening his shoulders, Bryce strode to the door and unlocked it. "Coming?" he asked tightly. Maybe if he ignored the incident, it would go away, just like the truck that was rapidly vanishing from sight.

Desha vacillated before she finally followed him into the house. Now it was too late to do anything about the truck anyway. The man was gone. Bryce had let him escape.

But the magic of the night was gone too. She and Bryce were at odds once again. The blue truck stood like a symbol of their differences.

She couldn't let the incident pass. "You should have trusted me and followed that truck," she said, right in the middle of the meal.

"And you shouldn't have even started that again," he returned. "Forget the truck. Forget the robber. We can't go through this every time we're together, every time you think you see someone or something that resembles the robber and the truck. Forget it."

"I won't," she said stubbornly. "Where's your support? Where's your sense of justice?"

"Let's try to enjoy your first evening in my home, shall we? he said tightly, wondering if that was possible now.

"By all means," she retorted.

But it was already too late. Bryce took Desha home early. The robber incident had spoiled all his plans for their first evening in his home. He would have given anything if that hadn't happened. He had planned to talk to Desha about their future.

By the time he returned to the house, he was more unhappy than ever. He couldn't stop thinking about the way Desha had looked at him, the things she had said. Had he been unfair? Or had she? Had he been so disappointed over the ruined romantic evening that he had lost his perspective? And did it even matter whose fault it was?

He took off his clothes and went to bed, but he couldn't sleep. He had wanted to discuss the future with Desha. He propped up in bed against the pillows and thought about how different his life was now that he had met her—chasing robbers, scaring the neighbors, hitting friends. It was all so crazy. Suddenly he laughed aloud.

In a blinding revelation, he saw the future without Desha, and he knew there was no point in *discussing* it. He couldn't imagine returning to his old staid and stuffy life, the barren tan world of his existence. He wanted to share Desha's madcap adventures. He wanted to spend his life with her. He wanted to give Elayne those grandchildren she wanted. He didn't care what the future brought as long as he could spend it with Desha.

He loved her. *That* was the crux of the matter. He had been fighting Cupid's arrow for all he was worth, but it had been a foolish fight.

He had to resist the urge to call Desha in the middle of the night and tell her how he felt. Tomorrow he would make a reservation at the most romantic restaurant in Virginia Beach, and invite Desha to dinner so that he could propose marriage—immediate marriage.

If she wouldn't agree to dinner, he would go to the shop and propose. If she wouldn't see him there, he would go to her hotel. However, he much preferred the restaurant he had in mind. He wanted it to be the most special night of her life—and his.

Desha had spent the night soul-searching. She knew that Bryce had lost all patience with her, and she had agonized over it, getting very little sleep. She would give anything if she could begin all over again, if she hadn't noticed the blue truck. She wanted to forget that she had ever seen that darned robber. Getting even with him wasn't worth losing Bryce. *Nothing* was worth that.

She realized that, in the long run, what mattered most was Bryce, not robbers or sun signs or success. She couldn't marry success. She was tired of traveling and searching and chasing dreams. She had found her destiny in the man she loved.

She got up, dressed and went about the motions of beginning her day, but she couldn't stop her mind from spinning. She began to formulate a plan. When she got to work, she would phone Bryce and apologize. She would tell him just exactly how she felt. She would not let pride stand in her way. It was much too late for that. She would tell him she loved him and take her chances.

All morning she walked around the shop, practicing what she would say to Bryce. She didn't want to sound reckless and rash. She wanted to explain that she loved him, and that nothing else mattered. He had said he was crazy about her. Surely there was a chance for them.

When she had finally gathered her nerve and readied her speech, she dialed Bryce's number only to find that it was busy. When she tried later, she received no answer at all. Her next impulse was to close the shop and try to find Bryce. But she didn't do that. She would wait until working hours were over. In the meantime, she would keep trying to reach him.

When the shop phone rang in the afternoon, Desha answered quickly. She hadn't been able to contact Bryce, but she had kept hoping he would call her.

"Good afternoon. *Southern Elegance*."

There was the slightest pause before Bryce spoke. "Hello, Desha."

"Hello, Bryce," she whispered.

"I'm sorry about last night," he said. "Will you forgive me and let me take you somewhere very special for dinner tonight to make up for it?"

"Oh, Bryce," she breathed, tears rushing to her eyes, "I'm sorry too. I'd love to go to dinner." She couldn't keep the elation from her voice. She had been so frantic, so frightened that he wouldn't want to see her again.

"I'll pick you up at seven-thirty."

"Fine," she said in an amazingly steady voice, but her hand was shaking when she put the phone down.

Rushing through the shop, Desha decided that she wanted to find something very special to wear. She wanted to look particularly nice tonight; she wanted to make up for last night.

At last she decided on a delicate pink dress with a high collar. It was rather demure, typical early *Southern Elegance*, but Desha liked the feminine way it made her feel. She spun around in front of the mirror, realizing for the first time what Elayne had meant by a certain look, a special look. With this dress, she felt that she had that look.

She wouldn't want to dress this way all the time, of course. But it felt just right for tonight.

The hours seemed to drag one by one until it was time for her to close the shop. She stayed until almost six-thirty, killing time. She was sure she would go mad if she had to sit idly in her hotel room while she waited for Bryce.

She was ready when he arrived, and so excited that she could hardly bear it. She had so many things she wanted to say to him.

She raced to the door and opened it to find Bryce dressed in a very stylish suit with a peach shirt and a bold rust tie. Desha had never seen him look more handsome.

For a moment, he couldn't seem to look away from her. "You are lovelier than ever," he murmured. "The dress is very becoming."

"Thank you, Bryce," she said, her heart beating rapidly. She wanted to blurt out everything to him, to tell him all the things on her mind and heart, but she restrained herself.

"You look very nice tonight yourself," she said.

He grinned. "Thank you. I went out and bought this today especially for the occasion." He looked down at the trendy suit and dressy shirt. "It's not my usual, is it? But I find that I rather like it for a change."

She laughed softly as she glanced down at her pink dress. "I know what you mean. I chose this in the shop today." Her eyes skimmed over his suit again. "It seems that we're a matched pair."

"Yes, it does doesn't it?" he murmured, his gaze holding hers. "Then you're ready?" He was eager to get under way.

They both fell silent on the way to the restaurant. When they got there, Desha told herself that she had never seen a more beautiful place. It was an old-fashioned mansion with three stories. She was pleased she had chosen to wear the pink dress.

After a young man came out to open her door and park the car, Bryce took her hand. "I hope you'll like the restaurant," he said, leading her up the steps of the magnificent stone building. He wanted her to remember this night for the rest of her life. *He* wanted to remember it, but only if she said yes to his marriage proposal.

"It's lovely, Bryce," she murmured. "Really special."

She felt like royalty when she and Bryce were led down the hall to an elegant dining room. The front faced a busy city street all lit up for the evening, but the back of the room overlooked the ocean. Desha thought it was the best of both worlds.

She had a heightened sense of anticipation as she and Bryce ordered wine, then selected their fare from the excellent seafood offerings on the menu. She sighed. She loved Virginia Beach. This was where she wanted to spend the rest of her life. She glanced across the table at Bryce. He was the man she wanted to spend her life with. Oh, if only *that* dream could come true.

Then, at last, the waiter was gone. Desha took a sip of her wine, then set it carefully on the starched white tablecloth. She could wait no longer.

"Desha," Bryce said, before she could speak, "there are so many things I want to say to you, and I might as well start with the most important. I love you. I want to marry you."

For a moment, Desha was too surprised to speak. This was more than she had dared dream. Bryce loved her! He wanted to marry her!

Bryce could feel his heart pound as he pulled a small white box out of his shirt pocket. "Will you marry me?" he asked.

He groaned at his impatience. Why couldn't he go about this night, of all nights, with his usual composure? Why did he feel like he would explode if he had to wait any longer to find out if she would be his bride? He lifted the family heirloom from the box and held it out to her.

"I know you see us as a bull and a ram," he said, "but surely you've heard the old saying that opposites attract. It will only make our love more intense, more wonderful."

"Oh, Bryce!" she cried, her voice filled with wonder. "The ring your mother wore."

"Say yes, Desha," he coaxed. "I want to share all your adventures. I want to spend the rest of my life showing you how much I love you."

Her eyes bright with tears of happiness, she tried to find the words she wanted to say to him, the words that had played in her head last night and today, but she was too overcome. She didn't see them as a bull and a ram, but only as a couple wonderfully in love. He was the only adventure she cared about. She looked out at the busy street, trying to compose herself so that she could tell him what was in her heart.

"Bryce, I know you think that I'm rash and irresponsible, but now that I've found the one dream that really matters to me—"

Suddenly, Bryce straightened in his chair and tossed his linen napkin down on the table. "I don't believe it!"

Desha stared at him in alarm. "You don't believe it?" she repeated in a tremulous voice.

"I'll be damned!" he exclaimed, pointing out the window. "It's your robber! And he *is* in the Crawfords' truck! I recognize him. He's one of their farm-hands.''

He shoved back his chair and stood up.

"Bryce, what are you doing?" Desha cried.

"I'm going after him. He'll not get away this time!" he declared. "Excuse me for a moment, will you, Desha?"

She couldn't believe her ears! Now *he* was chasing robbers, and at such a moment!

"Bryce!" she cried. "Don't!" She stood up and reached out to stop him. "You know where the robber can be found. Let the police take care of him."

He gazed at her frightened face. "I couldn't bear it if anything happened to you," she whispered. "Please don't go."

Suddenly, Bryce laughed softly and sat back down. "Yes, of course," he murmured, glancing around at the other diners, embarrassed now. "Calling the police is a more reasonable course of action. I don't know what got into me. When I saw that man in the Crawfords' truck and remembered your description of him, I could only think of dragging him out of that truck and holding him accountable."

"We'll call the police after dinner," she said gently, seating herself. "But right now we're in the middle of something much more important." Her glowing brown eyes met his. "Or don't you want to know what my answer is?"

He reached across the table and took her left hand in his. "More than anything in the world, but only if you say yes," he said, slipping the ring on her finger.

"It's so lovely," she murmured. "It looks like it caught the light of a hundred stars."

"Your stars," he said. "It's a sign, Desha. Do you remember when you told me that the stars hadn't yet lined up for you to marry?" He held her hand to his mouth and placed a tender kiss on her palm. "Well, now they have. Say that you'll be my bride."

"I want to marry you more than anything in the world, Bryce Gerrard," she whispered. "I love you so very much."

Bryce held her fingers to his lips again and kissed each one as he contemplated the years ahead with the woman fate had destined for his lifetime partner. Of course, Cupid hadn't made an error after all!

* * * * *

Silhouette Romance

COMING NEXT MONTH

#544 THAT'S WHAT FRIENDS ARE FOR—Annette Broadrick
Brad Crawford had once loved Penny Blackwell so much he'd been
willing to let her go. But now Brad was back and determined to save
Penny from marrying the wrong man. After all, to love, cherish and
protect—isn't that what friends are for?

#545 KANE AND MABEL—Sharon De Vita
Kati Ryan's diner was her pride and joy, so sparks flew when Lucas
Kane showed up, claiming to be her new partner. Luke needed a
change of scenery and Kati fit the bill—he'd show her they were both
born to raise Kane.

#546 DEAR CORRIE—Joan Smith
When it came to Bryan Holmes, columnist Corrie James knew she
should take her own advice—"no commitment, no dice." But this
romantic playboy was simply too sexy to resist!

#547 DREAMS ARE FOREVER—Joyce Higgins
Cade Barrett was investigating Leigh Meyers's company for
investment purposes, but in her he found a more valuable asset. He
wanted her for his own, but she'd given up on childhood dreams of
happy endings. He'd have to prove that dreams are forever....

#548 MID-AIR—Lynnette Morland
Whenever Lorelei Chant worked with pilot-producer Chris Jansen,
his sky-blue eyes made her heart soar. The trouble was, Chris seemed
to like flying alone. Could Lorelei convince him that love can happen
in the strangest places—even in mid-air?

#549 TOUCHED BY MAGIC—Frances Lloyd
Architect Alexandra Vickery's new client, Lucien Duclos, was quite a
handful—arrestingly attractive and extremely suspicious of women
designers. Alex was determined to prove herself, but how could she
keep her composure when she discovered he was as attracted to her as
she was to him?

AVAILABLE THIS MONTH:

ATTRACTIVE, SPACE SAVING BOOK RACK

Display your most prized novels on this handsome and sturdy book rack. The hand-rubbed walnut finish will blend into your library decor with quiet elegance, providing a practical organizer for your favorite hard-or soft-covered books.

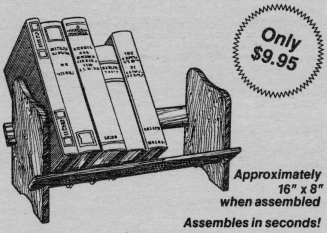

Only $9.95

Approximately 16" x 8" when assembled

Assembles in seconds!

To order, rush your name, address and zip code, along with a check or money order for $10.70* ($9.95 plus 75¢ postage and handling) payable to *Silhouette Books.*

Silhouette Books
Book Rack Offer
901 Fuhrmann Blvd.
P.O. Box 1396
Buffalo, NY 14269-1396

Offer not available in Canada.

BKR-2A

*New York and Iowa residents add appropriate sales tax.

In response
to last year's outstanding success,
Silhouette Brings You:

Silhouette Christmas Stories 1987

Specially chosen for you in a delightful volume celebrating the holiday season, four original romantic stories written by four of your favorite Silhouette authors.

Dixie Browning—*Henry the Ninth*
Ginna Gray—*Season of Miracles*
Linda Howard—*Bluebird Winter*
Diana Palmer—*The Humbug Man*

Each of these bestselling authors will enchant you with their unforgettable stories, exuding the magic of Christmas and the wonder of falling in love.

A heartwarming Christmas gift during the holiday season...indulge yourself and give this book to a special friend!

Available November 1987

XM87-1